Josephine Marie

Let no Man put Asunder

Josephine Marie

Let no Man put Asunder

ISBN/EAN: 9783337300197

Printed in Europe, USA, Canada, Australia, Japan

Cover: Foto ©Andreas Hilbeck / pixelio.de

More available books at **www.hansebooks.com**

Let No Man Put Asunder.

"ESPERANCE, HURRYING FORWARD, PLACED, WITH AN IM-
PULSE SHE DID NOT TRY TO RESIST, BOTH HANDS IN THE
OUTSTRETCHED ONES OF THE MAN WHO LOVED HER."

Let No Man Put Asunder.

BY

JOSEPHINE MARIÉ.

Author of "Love Stronger than Death," "Jeanne," etc.

NEW YORK, CINCINNATI, CHICAGO:

BENZIGER BROTHERS,

Printers to the Holy Apostolic See.

1898

CONTENTS.

LET NO MAN PUT ASUNDER.

CHAPTER I.

THE HOSPITAL.

"AH, there you are, Doctor!" exclaimed nurse Agnes, as a middle-aged man with iron-gray hair and mustache met her at the door of a private ward in one of the long corridors of a city hospital.

"Have you told her?" she asked, lowering her voice.

"Not yet; but," he added cheerily and aloud, so that the patient within could hear him, "I am going this moment to propose our little plan to Mademoiselle. I trust she is stronger this bright day." And as he entered the room, the nurse with ready tact withdrew.

I   7

There is something dreary about a hospital ward, however neat and fresh it may be, and it struck the physician painfully as he crossed the threshold with a quick glance at the fragile form in the small bedstead near the window, where a single rose was striving its best to breathe a little of its own sweetness into the sick-chamber.

" Well, how is my patient this morning? I hope our conversation of yesterday was not too much for that little brain, eh, Mam'selle? How did you sleep last night?"

" Better, much better, thank you." And even in those few words a less attentive listener than the worthy man beside her would have noticed at once the peculiar sweetness of the voice and the foreign accent which betrayed the French nationality of the young speaker.

" Good! I want that small head to be particularly clear this morning; clear enough to perceive at once the reasonableness and urgency of a plan I have been weaving since some days past ;—I and my wife," he added cautiously. "Do you think you can guess what it is?"

"I fear I am not quick at guessing conundrums, Monsieur le docteur," she replied, smiling and shaking her head.

"Well, it is very simple, even if difficult to guess—very simple. I am just going to take you, bag and baggage, home with me to-day. Listen, Espérance," he said earnestly, noting her startled look, and calling her for the first time by name, all the pretended gruffness leaving his voice, which grew wonderfully gentle. "You remember, do you not, how I spoke the other day of the little girl we lost years ago, leaving a void in our home in spite of our two dear-boys? Had she lived, she would have been just your age. We—my wife and I—want you to come and help fill that void, to be as long as you will, our daughter. Will you come?"

But for a moment Espérance Le Clerque could not answer. Touched inexpressibly,

she was for an instant speechless with wonder and emotion.

"Oh, Monsieur," she murmured, after
that first involuntary silence, "how can I?
how can I? Why, you do not even know
who we—who I am." The little correction
spoke volumes to the physician, who, a few
weeks before, had witnessed the death-parting
between the mother and child. "Monsieur
—ah, you are too kind, too good!"

"Nonsense, my dear. I know you well
enough to be quite sure that you have crept
into this old heart of mine, and that is more
than sufficient. Some time, when you are
stronger, you can tell me, if you will, more of
your poor mother's history; but in the meanwhile we must get you home. There is no
time to be lost, for the hospital is becoming
crowded, and you might be compelled at any
hour to share this room with others—something you could not endure in your present
nervous condition."

"Could I not be moved to some—some

boarding-place?" she asked bravely. " I
have a little money, Monsieur, and will soon
be able to teach or——"

"And do you think, my dear child, a
young, beautiful girl like you—only seven-
teen, I think you told me—could go alone
to some strange boarding-place in this big
metropolis of New York, even were you
well, without some sort of protector, some
one to give you an aiding hand?"

"Perhaps Father Searlington, my kind
friend——"

"Father Searlington is absolutely power-
less to help you in that way, however kind a
friend he may be. Zounds! what an obsti-
nate head for such young shoulders," pur-
posely resuming his gruffness of manner.
"Now, I don't want any more objections.
You would die if you remained here longer;
you cannot find for the present any fitting
dwelling outside; and how long, I would
like to know, would a few hundred dollars
last?" Then, as he saw how white the fair

face grew, he said tenderly: "I understand all that you feel, but you must not
regard us as strangers; we are friends sent
you, not only for your own sake, but for their
own"; and with touch as gentle as a woman's
he smoothed the tumbled hair lying carelessly across the pillow. "I will come for
you at four this afternoon to bring you home.
It must be home to you, dearest child, till—
till you get tired of us," he added, laughing,
though there was a suspicious moisture in
the kind eyes keenly watching each change
of the mobile face. "Remember, at four."

"Yes, Monsieur," she answered softly.
And nurse Agnes, coming to the door a
little later, found her resting quietly, her
lips half parted in a smile; and by them was
a small ivory crucifix, as though the little
emblem of mercy had been pressed to them
in thanksgiving.

CHAPTER II.

" Now, boys, I want everything as cheery as possible," said Mrs. Thornsdale, an elderly woman, whose pleasant voice and gentle face, framed in by a dainty cap of white lace, somehow suggested at once the winning appellation—motherly.

The boys, as she' called them—the elder fully six feet in height, the other scarcely shorter—rose eagerly to greet her as, descending the light wood staircase, she joined them in the square hall, which, with divan and big cushions, a large lamp with crimson snade beside an upright piano, formed in itself a room christened by common consent " the Den."

" Well, you are just in your element, little mother," said the younger son, placing his

13

arm affectionately around her. "You are never so happy as when playing the part of the good Samaritan. I am not at all sure that your philanthropy in this case will prove rich in reward, however fair the stranger may be."

"Are you not ashamed, Anselm!" exclaimed Mrs. Thornsdale. "Poor motherless girl! My heart goes out to her. Just think of her being left suddenly alone in this strange city; so young, too—not eighteen, I believe." But she looked very tenderly at the boyish, well-knit form as Anselm began half playing, half drumming on the piano.

"What is it to be, mother mine?" asked Donaldson, fifteen months the senior of his brother—who was just twenty-one,—carelessly striking a few chords on a banjo. "Will a jig or a waltz suit your small majesty?"

"Now, don't tease, Donald, there's a dear. Just——" but there was no time to finish the sentence, for the key was heard fumbling in the latch, the cheery voice of the doctor talking quickly as he always did when excited. An instant later, throwing the door wide open, he entered, the slender, girlish form of Espérance clinging to his arm.

"There! we have caught the bird at last, mother," he said, laughing; "and a precious difficult bird it was to catch,—a frozen one, too, I guess. Zounds, how cold it is!"

"Well, as long as we have the bird, that is all we wish. Welcome, a thousand times, my dear child"; and drawing Espérance to her, she kissed her so tenderly that the girl's heart warmed to her at once. "You are cold; you must come and warm yourself by the open fire. This is Anselm, our youngest son," she said, as the latter came hastily forward to greet her. But the elder brother would have slipped away, could he have done so unobserved, for with instinctive thoughtfulness he feared it would be bewildering to the young stranger to meet so many at once.

"This is Donaldson," Dr. Thornsdale was

already saying,—" Dr. Donaldson Thurston Thornsdale that is to be," he added pompously.

"I am very glad to know you," said Espérance shyly; but the sweet voice was quite clear, and Donald thought he had never seen anything more pathetic or winning than the half-pleading, grateful light in the dark eyes raised timidly to his, which even in that first moment of greeting seemed to him the mirror of a beautiful soul.

CHAPTER III.

ESPÉRANCE TELLS THE STORY OF HER MOTHER'S LIFE.

"OH, the poor honey, the poor honey! If she ain't a goner, my name is not Dinah."

Dinah, whose mother had been the faithful "Mammy" in Mrs. Thornsdale's southern home, was expressive, if not elegant, upon every occasion, and was far from being the least important personage in the doctor's household.

The strain and excitement had been too much for Espérance's feeble strength, and, as the physician anticipated, as soon as she reached her room she fainted.

"That's right, Dinah; rub her hands. She will revive in a few minutes," exclaimed the doctor, too concerned just then to heed

2   17

her quaint expression of sympathy and alarm.

"She's comin' to already, I declar' to goodness, Missus," she said, greatly relieved, a moment later, as Mrs. Thornsdale entered the room with salts and ammonia. "The color is comin' into her cheeks, for all the world like the pink gleam in a rose-leaf"; and the black face above the fragile one on the pillow fairly beamed with admiration and delight.

"Did I faint?" murmured Espérance, as she opened her eyes, a little dazed. "How stupid of me! I am sorry to give so much trouble," with a smile that went straight to the negress' heart.

"Not at all stupid to do the most natural thing in the world," answered Dr. Thornsdale in his abrupt way. "Only you must be an obedient child, and let the little mother put you at once to bed; and I will return soon to see whether my orders have been obeyed."

"This is our faithful Dinah, who has been with us for years," said Mrs. Thornsdale, as her husband left the room. "You must not hesitate to call her for anything you need, dear child."

"I am sure it will be very nice to have her," replied Espérance in her sweet way, as she held her hand out by way of greeting, thus unconsciously making the negress from that instant her devoted slave.

"It looks just like a pearl in a heap of coal-dust," thought Dinah, as she looked at the small hand in her big black one; but she only smiled blandly, showing a dazzling row of large, well-shaped teeth, and mumbled something about being happy "to minister to such a nice Miss Honey" (Dinah always used the biggest words she could think of—"more expressive-like to do so," she once remarked). And before long Espérance was resting quiet, if exhausted, in the snowy bed with its muslin curtains, that looked so dainty amid the cretonne furnishings of the room.

The next day, though still feeble, she insisted upon telling the doctor and his wife the sad story of her mother's life.

"My great-grandfather was le Comte Ducet. My grandparents dying when Maman (she always pronounced the tender name with the French intonation) was a very young child, she was left to the sole guardianship of the Comte, a stern old man, proud to a fault of his ancestral name and estates, though the latter had shrunk greatly in value since the Reign of Terror, remaining, however, quite large in extent. I believe the old Comte loved Maman as much as a cold and selfish nature would permit; but his pride in the beauty and talents of which she gave evidence at an early age amounted to a passion. Having no direct male heir, his ambition centred entirely in her—'la petite Pauline,' she was called by the few friends who visited the castle from time to time. He would dream of the future when she would make a brilliant marriage, and perhaps one day have a son who eventually might bear the title, so that the old name might not die. But, alas for him! and for her too, perhaps (my poor Maman!), his castle-in-the-air was to vanish in thinnest vapor. When she was scarcely eighteen—just my age—her grandfather engaged as drawing-master an Englishman fifteen years her senior. He was handsome, clever, a gentleman in every sense of the word, and he soon fell desperately in love with his pupil—seemed to, at least," added Espérance with a sigh. "Maman more than returned his affection. To her he seemed all that was good and noble. Well, it was the story one hears so often. After fruitless pleading on her part, and more than one stormy interview between her guardian and her artist-lover, she consented to be secretly married." The girl paused a second, the ticking of the clock heard distinctly in the silence.

"She did not tell her grandfather till—till it was necessary to do so. She was frightened, but hopeful, for she believed he loved her too well to be very cruel just when she most needed tenderness. But she was mistaken. In words of unpardonable brutality he told her that he did not so much as believe in her marriage; that, even did it exist, he would never sanction such a *mésalliance* (to such an unbending aristocrat it seemed that), or pardon such hypocrisy. In vain my mother pleaded, reminding him that both she and Reginald (my father's name, you know) had spoken to him of their wishes; that it was his sternness alone which had caused them to be wedded clandestinely. It but angered him the more. An hour later my father found her lying outstretched upon the ground, just outside of the gates of her old home—unconscious."

"For a year," she continued bravely, though

her voice faltered now, " in spite of humiliat-
ing struggles which followed, and moments of
remorse as she thought of the loneliness of
the old Comte, who, whatever his faults had
been, had educated and sheltered her from
childhood, Maman knew what it was to be
very happy.   My father, touched perhaps at
first by the love which had sacrificed everything for him, for a while captivated by her
beauty, seemed devoted to her.   And when I
came, and she knew, as she once said to me,
that she had a little life all her own to cherish, her heart was full of happiness ; and, calling me her tiny harbinger of hope, she named
me Espérance.

" In less than a year from that day he for
whom she had given up home, kindred, and
fortune had fled —why, or where, she never
knew."

The tender voice faltered utterly then, but
she controlled herself instantly.

" Waiting and searching in vain, weeks flew
by.   Her thoughts turned instinctively to her

grandfather, but she knew it would be worse
than useless to appeal to him.   More than
ever would he disbelieve the story of her marriage, now that her husband had deserted her;
and the memory of his brutal words made her
sensitive nature shrink from exposing herself
a second time to such cruel insult.

" My father had occasionally spoken of a
maiden aunt who lived in one of the suburbs
of London; and Maman determined to seek
her, dimly hoping to find some clew of him
there.   The aunt received her kindly; but
bluntly, though without roughness, told my
poor dear mother the past record of the one
whose name she bore—a past so shameful that
Maman would never speak of it in detail to
me.   She stayed in England for some years,
supporting us both by teaching French and
music, occasionally drawing; and it was there
I learned to speak English when a mere child.
Homesick for la belle France, she took me,
when about seven years old, back to her own
sunny land she loved so dearly, and placed

me at the convent of the Sacré Cœur in Paris,
where she knew that, side by side with a complete secular education, I would be taught the
truths of religion—a teaching which she herself had had slight opportunity of obtaining,
for the old Comte had been more of an atheist
than anything else. The convent was near
my mother's dwelling; and she often said that
her daily visit each evening to me was her
rest and recreation after the working hours of
the day. Gradually the gentle influence of
the dear nuns, their tender sympathy, melted
the ice around my poor mother's heart, and
for the first time in all those years of bitterness she learned peace—for she found Him
who promised that the weary and heavy-laden
should find rest in Him."

The face of the young speaker lighted with
loving reverence, as the last words died in a
whisper.

" Did your mother never hear of her grandfather, even indirectly, my child?" asked the
doctor.

"She received news of his death only through the newspapers, about five years after my birth, and upon inquiry learned that he had willed everything to a distant relative whom he had scarcely seen. About a year ago," she continued after a pause, "Maman, knowing that I would have to work my own way in the world, thought I would have perhaps more advantages here than abroad; so we came, our only friend in this big country being the kind Jesuit Father of whom you have heard me speak, Father Searlington, who had been ordered to this country shortly before we sailed; the only friend till I found—you. Oh, Monsieur, how good you all are to me! So good that I think Maman herself must have sent you to me."

The simple faith of the words was touching, and went straight to the kindly hearts listening to them.

"You must rest now, dearie," said Mrs. Thornsdale, bending to kiss her. "Try to sleep, will you not?"

"We must ask this Father Scarlington to come and see her," the doctor said to his wife as they left the room, closing the door softly after them. "It will make her feel less strange. He has known her since she was a very young child—poor, brave, little girl."

CHAPTER IV

WITHIN a few weeks of her arrival at the Thornsdales' it was Espérance's eighteenth birthday, and the doctor puzzled his brain striving to make the day less sad for her. A thought suddenly suggesting itself, he hailed an omnibus, and in a few moments reached the rectory in West 16th Street. An expression of keen pleasure lighted Father Searlington's face as, hastily adjusting his glasses, he read the card just handed him by the brother:

"Dr. Anselm Thornsdale."

" Say I will be down at once," and a minute later he descended the wide staircase, suggesting forcibly the portraits of Dante, a long cloak hanging in loose folds from his shoulders. Over six feet, slender, with classic

28

head crowned by jet-black hair tinged with
the purplish hue which gave to the blackness
an added richness; a perfectly shaped and
slightly wavy beard of the same color, causing the almost marble whiteness of the skin
and deep-set eyes to stand out with startling
contrast, Father Searlington was altogether
an unusually striking as well as intellectual-
looking man.

Dr. Thornsdale's own gray eyes flashed
with pleased surprise as he noted in a glance
every detail of the commanding figure of the
Jesuit, as he crossed the threshold to greet
him, in the alert yet stately way characteristic to him.

"This is an unexpected pleasure, Dr.
Thornsdale. I am delighted to have this opportunity of meeting the kind friend of Mlle.
Le Clerque," for he at once surmised that
it was regarding Espérance that the doctor
had called.

"The pleasure is mutual," replied the
latter in his hearty way. "And I am going

to ask you to waive all ceremony by coming around to dine with us this evening. Quite *en famille*, I assure you," he hastened to add, seeing the priest hesitate. " Poor little Mam'selle is sad to-day; it is her birthday, you know, and I felt sure that the surprise of seeing her 'best friend,' as she calls you, would do more to cheer her than anything else."

" I have found a formidable rival to dispute that title with me now," replied the priest, with ready courtesy, smiling. " I fear it will be impossible for me to accept this evening. I have——"

" Now don't tell me you cannot come. I have set my heart upon giving the child the surprise of bringing you around with me. We dine at half after six, and it is just six now, is it not?" he said, inquiringly, as the Angelus bell was heard just then.

" Yes, pardon me a moment," and leaving him for a few minutes, Father Searlington returned, saying that he could accept the invitation, as one of the other Fathers had consented to attend to a matter for him that evening.

"What do you think of Mlle. Le Clerque's health?" he asked Dr. Thornsdale as they walked leisurely up-town. "I am deeply interested in her, having known her since childhood. I knew her mother well, a noble and much-injured woman. You know something of her history, do you not?"

"Yes; Espérance told us. A sad story indeed, and the child's own future promises to be one of struggle also. Well, one thing is certain: she is in no condition to undertake work of any kind for some time to come. Her system is completely shattered. Our plan would be to keep her with us, to have her make her home with us indefinitely, and I wish you would exert your influence to make her see things in this light."

"I will do my best," replied the priest; "but if I mistake not, Mam'selle's high spirit will rebel so much against utter inaction and

the sense of being—you will excuse my
speaking frankly——"

"I understand, I understand," interrupted
the doctor, "the sense of dependence."

"Exactly. A feeling she cannot avoid,
however kind and considerate you and your
wife are. It seems to me, therefore, that if
she were to procure pupils for French or
drawing (she has remarkable talent for the
latter, inherited I suppose from the father),
as soon as it is at all feasible, still remaining
under the shelter of your home, as you are
good enough to offer, her nervous system
would be benefited and her general health
better for having the definite interest and
occupation. Work is a great panacea in
time of trouble, however much it may seem
to be at times the contrary."

"There is much truth in what you say,".
replied the physician meditatively. "Labor,
though laid upon mankind as a punishment,
has proved a blessing instead of a curse in
more ways than one."

"A beautiful proof of the Almighty's goodness in tempering everything penal in life with merciful compensations. Mlle. Espérance will of course be guided by your decision."

"Later, work in moderation, I will heartily advise, but at present it is out of the question. She has been well trained intellectually; is fully competent to teach, and when stronger can do so, remaining under our guardianship. I was amused at the quick way she replied to a lady a day or two ago, who was defending Darwinism and ended by saying she would never accept anything on faith; it would be too unintelligent, particularly in this age. 'But, Madame,' responded Espérance, 'you have just admitted that in evolution there is not one, but numerous gaps to be filled, yet you believe without doubt that not one, but every, missing link will be at last traced sooner or later; is not that making many acts of faith?' Poor lady, she was quite discomfited."

3

" Mam'selle has a clear mind," replied the priest with a benevolent smile, "quite in touch with the spirit of the century as far as inquiry is concerned — this 'age which blots out life with question-marks,' according to Lowell. Well, I thoroughly believe in investigating everything."

"You do not fear the researches of science, then?"

"Certainly not; why should I?" asked the Jesuit, surprised. "One truth cannot contradict another, religious or otherwise. There is no fact fully demonstrated by science which jars ever so slightly with any Christian fact or doctrine, revealed or historical. The absolute demonstrations of science have helped instead of hindered our cause, by proving from even a mere human standpoint the authenticity of certain facts narrated in Scripture. Take the Deluge, for example. Formerly infidels laughed at the assertion, and asked where sufficient water to cover the globe could have originated.

Geologists now point to a time when the earth must have been covered with water, and prove from the striæ and abrasions observed on mountains that there existed a glacial period when a great part of the world was covered with immense glaciers several thousand feet in depth, that provided water for a universal deluge, which they say occurred, involving a revolution in all parts of the globe. No," said Father Searlington, "it is only some unproved assertions of certain so-called scientific men that clash with any positive teaching of Christianity. That I would vouch for without hesitation. Among even the unproved scientific theories there is matter which could be reconciled to Scriptural assertions. Undoubtedly," he added, "there are certain traditions affecting neither doctrinal nor moral truth which, in common with antiquity at large, the Church has tacitly accepted as true, which in time may be proved erroneous."

"Such as the revolving of the sun around

the earth, in the time of Galileo, I suppose," replied Dr. Thornsdale, with a shrewd glance.

" Exactly.   The Bible is not an inspired record so far as cosmogony or geology is concerned, nor has it ever been defined as such in any era by any *ex-cathedra* utterance of the Church.   Galileo was condemned, not for his theory as a scientific probability, but for not keeping the question of religion aloof from his philosophical speculations regarding the question at stake.   Nusa and Copernicus had both held that the earth revolved around the sun, and enjoyed the friendship and confidence of the highest dignitaries of the Church.   Nusa was made cardinal, and Copernicus, when unable to give his great work on the subject to the world on account of the attendant cost, was enabled to do so eventually through the munificence of Cardinal Schonberg.   Galileo, you know, went so far as to assert that portions of the Scripture could not be satisfactorily explained unless his theory was admitted. His prison, by the way, during his trial of ten months' duration, was the palace of the Tuscan ambassador, and afterward the charming Villa Ascetri, near the church where his two daughters were nuns, whom he frequently visited."

"Well, all these discussions should be productive of much good," said the doctor, thoughtfully. "But here we are," as they approached a brown-stone house near Madison Square. "If I mistake not, there is Mam'selle herself in the window looking like a veritable ghost."

But the "ghost" could claim no right to the title, even were she desirous of doing so, as she came eagerly forward to greet them, her face flushed with delighted surprise. Not only Mrs. Thornsdale, but the young men, were charmed with the Jesuit, who, combining the manners and knowledge of a man of the world with the kindliness and dignity of the priest, adapted himself to each with easy tact and grace, the young orphan passing a bright evening in spite of the lingering sadness of associations called forth by her first birthday in a strange home.

CHAPTER V.

THE TWO BROTHERS.

WEEKS passed into months full of varied experience for Espérance as she slowly recuperated from the fever which had laid her low at the hospital.

As Father Searlington anticipated, she insisted so firmly upon beginning work of some kind that it was useless to oppose her, and within a few months she had obtained several pupils, to whom she gave drawing and French lessons in the cosy library of the Thornsdales' city house. Her winning nature, so gentle and gay, yet so serious, endeared her more and more to both the doctor and his wife, making them unwilling to part with her, while Donald and Anselm vied with each other in making her feel at home. The brothers, alike in a few respects, were very different in others. Anselm had a gay, light-hearted way about him which, combined with an unusually handsome face, with light-brown hair and laughing blue eyes, attracted every one at once. Donald, on the contrary, was quieter and had the reputation of being very reserved. Darker and taller than the former, he resembled his father. He had the same keen, kind gray eyes, the high, intellectual forehead, the firm mouth and chin of the doctor—altogether a singularly strong, rather than beautiful, countenance, whereas Anselm, in spite of a firm-set chin, had a rather irresolute expression about his mouth, suggestive of latent weakness of character. One felt that his was a colder, more calculating nature than his brother's, but that, were he once aroused, his passion for good or evil might be limitless. Donaldson's was one of those deep characters that, capable of loving with a love unto death, would ever be master of its higher nature,

ready to make whatever sacrifice affection
or duty might demand. Anselm, though fond
of society and enjoying the admiration his
charm of manner and face evoked, particularly among women, preferred, like Donald, the society of men rather than that of
the fairer sex.

He was, however, keenly sensitive to the
world's opinion from every aspect, and would
twit Donald about his utter indifference to
the sayings of " Mrs. Grundy." " You are
the Diogenes of the family, Don," he would
say, teasingly. " Had you lived in the Al-
exandrian age, you might have consented to
live in something more prosaic than a tub,
but you would have been as superior as
he to the petty follies of the day." But
much as he admired his brother, he was
well satisfied with himself. Humility,
essential to a really great character, he
absolutely lacked. Intelligent, and like
Donald fond of athletics and of certain
lines of study, with a heart not naturally

unkind, though selfish, generous to a fault in money matters, enjoying nothing better than giving his friends a good time, as he expressed it, and boasting of a high sense of honor in little as well as in great things, Anselm Thornsdale was undoubtedly a young man of many good impulses, with a peculiar fascination which Espérance readily recognized.

His overflowing spirits and boyish ways amused her, and she felt from the first at her ease with him; yet it was Donald's deeper nature and more delicate attention which secretly appealed to her, and after the first shyness wore away, it was to him she spoke of her inner life, her mother's sad history. Not until later did she realize how she had grown to depend upon his quiet sympathy and sound advice, his unerring thoughtfulness of her in every detail, the strong, clear mind and heart ever quick to pity and shelter the weak and helpless, whether poor or rich, of high station or low.

As for Donald himself, the whole strength of his chivalrous nature went out to the orphan girl, so gentle and diffident, yet so brave amid the sadness of her bereavement and the new circumstances under which she had been placed. She won him more each day, and in after-life he always asserted that from the first moment he had looked into her noble face she had become his queen, the dear empress of his heart, whose purity was to be his light, even when deepest darkness enveloped both him and her.

CHAPTER VI.

THE THORNSDALE COUNTRY-SEAT.

THE early part of June the Thornsdales moved to their country-seat on the Hudson, not far from West Point. The grounds were quite extensive, and the old-fashioned house seemed almost buried beneath lilac and wild-rose bushes. It was a quaint, picturesque place. The house itself was over a hundred and twenty-five years old, with winding passages and rambling rooms full of interest to the young girl, who seemed to enjoy her own difficulty in finding her way about when she first entered the old homestead, laughing at her own stupidity, as she called it, in invariably turning to the left instead of to the right, or *vice versa*. The library was the delight of her heart. It consisted of two

44

large, square rooms, seeming like one when
the portières were thrown back; the walls
were lined with shelves of numerous books
well classified, and in the corner was a great
open fire-place, a large iron kettle swinging
over the logs, the high mantle of olden times
rising above, with odd inscriptions engraven
in clay beneath.

"I do not feel as if I were living in the
prosaic nineteenth century," she said to
Anselm one day. "It seems as if I were
the heroine of a novel, as if I must expect to
hear, at any instant, horses' hoofs galloping
by with men equipped for battle, stopping at
this delightful old homestead for a moment's
refreshment."

"A Napoleon among them, for instance,"
was the teasing reply.

"Indeed, I would not object in the least
to welcoming his Napoleonic majesty—provided he was my friend," she added with a
little laugh. "Seriously, in spite of my
admiration for him as a flashing, picturesque

character in history, I think there is no
military leader more disappointing or tan-
talizing than Napoleon; none whom I, in
some ways, respect less. He was a provok-
ing mixture of good and bad qualities, force
and weakness."

"Well, I admire him in every way," answered Anselm, impulsively. "The man
seemed born to command, to accomplish
whatever he undertook to do. At the age of
fourteen, when speaking with enthusiasm of
Marshal Turenne to some lady with whom
he was conversing, he defended his action of
burning the Palatinate, exclaiming: 'What
mattered it since it was necessary to the
success of his plan?' That speech of .
. Napoleon at fourteen was characteristic of
his own indomitable will, which would sweep
everything before him."

"Except Waterloo," replied the girl,
parenthetically. "And do you admire him
for sacrificing everything sacred or profane
to his own ambition?" she asked, gravely.

" Had he been disinterestedly devoted to the glory of his country, he would have been grander morally, grander in every way. True patriotism ennobles a character. France and Napoleon, not France alone, was his battle-cry."

" One should not, of course, sacrifice principle for any cause," rejoined Anselm, noting her shocked expression. " But I can easily understand being carried away at some supreme moment when some longed-for object was to be wrenched from one."

" He did not hesitate to sacrifice even poor Josephine, who, whatever her faults were, was at least devoted to him," Espérance said, musingly, not pleased at Anselm's words.

" That is something which has always puzzled me, by the way. I thought your Church never sanctioned divorces."

" Neither does it. When the marriage has been valid, nothing can dissolve the tie."

" Napoleon divorced Josephine?"

"True; but without the sanction of the Church. The Diocesan tribunal, which, by the bye, was not composed of bishops, as Thiers erroneously asserts, to which he had successful recourse for the annulment of his union with Josephine, was illegal, incompetent in those particular premises to pronounce judgment upon so important a question. It had no authority in a case like that, a fact of which Napoleon must have been aware, ignoring as he did the existence of the Pope, whom he must have known was the proper judge in such matters. Yet even that sycophantic tribunal did not attempt to dissolve the tie without first pronouncing that the marriage had been invalid from the very beginning."

"And did the Church eventually agree with that decision?"

"No. The Church regarded the union as valid. Napoleon from the first had been tricky. Before he was to be crowned as Emperor, Josephine began to have qualms of conscience regarding her union with Napoleon, and to satisfy her, he demanded his uncle, Cardinal Fesch, to perform a religious ceremony privately, representing to him that, owing to the necessity of secrecy and lack of time, the ordinary rules of canon law then existent in France of having at least two witnesses, and the ceremony performed by the pastor of either one of the contracting parties, must be dispensed with. But the cardinal, seeing through the scheme, and being conscientious, had immediate recourse to the Pope, obtaining from him the required dispensation. The Pope, being the source of canon law, had of course the right to give any necessary dispensation regarding minor particulars which in their own nature would not invalidate the Sacrament. *Voilà tout, Monsieur;* there is the whole case in few words."

"What, discussing Napoleon again!" said Donaldson, entering the room just then. "An entirely too warm day for arguments,

4

I should say. Do you not want to drive
with me instead, Espérance? It is glorious
outdoors." And shortly after, she and
Donald, in the dogcart, were speeding along
the beautiful road by the river, Espérance
not sorry to leave Anselm, whose words
had left an uncomfortable impression.

CHAPTER VII.

IT was difficult to say which of the brothers Espérance saw most frequently when they first moved to "Lalla Rookh," the odd name with which the doctor had christened the old homestead, partly from admiration of Moore's genius, partly because the title was unique. Gradually, however, it became an acknowledged fact that it was Donaldson who would drive her every Sunday to the little church at the Point, sometimes in time for the late service, or again in the early morning when hill and field and flower were blushing beneath the first touch of dawn; Donaldson, who would shower her with delicate attentions which no one else would think of, and who

51

would steal time from his studies, at least
on Saturdays, to go for a long drive or walk
with her at his side.

Occasionally on Sundays he would go in
to the service with her. As a boy, he had
followed with sincerity the belief of his
mother, who was an Episcopalian, but as he
grew to manhood he lost faith in any definite
creed. His nature was too deep, however,
to allow him ever to become irreverent, or
in any way irreligious, and he was quick to
appreciate Espérance's devotion to her religion, which entered into every detail of
her life. Her intelligent explanation of its
doctrines and ceremonials interested him,
while the logic and consistency of all that
she believed appealed to his practical mind.

Anselm had never been religious, even as
a child, and as he became older he rarely
gave a definite or serious thought to anything
pertaining to religion—more perhaps from
indifference than from any motive. He
seemed utterly to lack appreciation of the

supernatural. To be eminently respectable, and a gentleman in every sense of the word, was about the substance of his creed, though if any one had given him such definition as a synopsis of his individual views, he would doubtless have been surprised—very much surprised—if any one had ventured to say that mere respectability in itself was incapable of opening the portals of a happy future existence. Espérance gave him credit for deeper feeling in such matters, but she rarely discussed the tenets of her Church unless asked to explain some point; she did what was far better, she lived her faith.

Donald was to sail in September for a three years' course of study at the medical universities of Paris and Germany, and he dreaded the enforced separation from the companionship daily becoming dearer to him. Well, he was a worker by nature, and his love would but give added inspiration to both labor and study, he tenderly mused; when he returned he would have a future to offer worthy, if possible, even of her, so earnestly would he work for her.

Thinking only of what was best and right for her, he resolved not to speak till he had full right to do so. She was young, had seen nothing of the world, and was in so delicate a position in their household, notwithstanding that her earnings from teaching were rendering her gradually quite independent in a pecuniary way, that he shrank from seeming to take even involuntary advantage of her gratitude and inexperience by influencing her future life by a declaration of his affection and ardent hopes. The very strength of his love made him consider only her best interests. But he saw that her face brightened at his approach as it did at no other's coming; that she was always happy to be with him, and it was hard to keep silent.

Dr. Thornsdale noted his deepening affection, and at first feared it might be unreciprocated. He understood his boy too

well not to know that love with Donaldson
would be no light thing; but a hundred
so-called nothings reassured him, and he
began to build bright dreams for a happy
future when he might welcome his ward
as daughter in very truth.

He spoke of his conviction and hopes to
his wife; but she only laughed and told him
he was a dear, inveterate, old matchmaker,
who wanted every one to be happy as they
had been. And with tender interest they
watched together the eager, beautiful face
of Espérance, who was talking at the end of
the room with Donaldson, discussing plans
for the children's tableaux she was impro-
vising for the benefit of a poor little church
not far from Lalla Rookh.

CHAPTER VIII.

THE CHILDREN'S TABLEAUX.

IT was the evening of the tableaux, and the hall was crowded.

"Comin' through the Rye" was presented by a charming little couple, who, in spite of being able to boast of only a dozen summers, seemed quite to enter into the arch spirit of the pretty scene, while a chorus of young voices sang the ballad in the distance.

"Jack Horner" followed, much to the bliss of the small boy of six who impersonated the Mother-Goose character, and who showed his appreciation of at least the plum by devouring it before the curtain went down, much to the amusement of every one, the tiny actor himself included, who beamed with pride as the audience loudly applauded.

Eight pictures followed, each thoroughly original as well as artistic; but the crowning success of the evening was the minuet.

Demurely and gracefully a miniature marquise with hair grown mysteriously white, and dainty gown of figured satin, with coquettish slippers to match, courtesied low to a miniature marquis in knee-breeches of velvet and gorgeous coat, adorned with lace, the powdered wig with knotted ribbons making him royal indeed, a three-cornered hat with yellow plumes set daintily on his head, or sweeping the floor as he bowed with courtly grace to the little lady of ancient days.

Never, Donald and Anselm agreed, did Espérance seem more winning than when she was surrounded a little later by a group of the excited children, each trying to vie with the other in saying what fun they had had, which they thought was the prettiest, etc.

"Oh, I just love being marquised," said a small urchin of nine. "Won't you please keep on marquising me, Miss Espérance?"

"Ah, I am afraid you would get tired of such finery all the time," replied Espérance, laughing. "I am afraid cycles and other things, to say nothing of football, would have to be dispensed with in such gorgeous attire. Ah, Edgar, there you are," as "Jack Horner," minus plum, made a rush to kiss her. "Did you have fun too, and which did you think the very prettiest and greatest success of all?"

"Myself," was the proud reply. And as this, to say the least, complacent and ready answer created a general laugh, he looked puzzled and rather hurt for a second, but decided to join the merriment he had aroused, without understanding why.

"They are clapping almost as much as when I was on the stage, aren't they?" he whispered with delight.

"And I think it is this which is the

loveliest of all," said a familiar voice close
by; and Espérance, looking up, saw Anselm
watching her with an expression of such
keen admiration that she flushed involuntarily.

"Nonsense," she murmured lightly.
"Good-night, children. Oh, don't smother
me, dears," she said, laughing, as they all
gathered close to her, clamoring for a good-by
kiss; "you must leave just a little bit of me,
just to show that I lived once, you know."

"Ain't Miss Espérance a trump?" exclaimed one of the boys, as she disappeared.
"I say, Jim," he whispered to one of the
small actors beside him, "I think he is
'mashed' on her, don't you?"

"Shouldn't be surprised if both was,"
was the ungrammatical rejoinder of this ex-
marquis, as the tall form of Donald was seen
standing beside her and Anselm, as she
waited for her wraps.

"The trap is waiting," Donaldson was saying as he joined them. "Are you able to

make your escape with safety from this miniature Babel?"

"Just a moment for my wraps," replied Espérance. "Are you not coming with us also, Anselm?"

"Your mother is waiting for you in the carriage, Anselm. Hurry!" called the doctor's loud voice just then; but the son frowned as he obeyed the summons. "Always Donald," he muttered impatiently, as his brother helped the girl into the buggy; nor did he analyze why he should have felt suddenly irritated.

Espérance, elated with the success of the evening's entertainment, was in high spirits as she and Donaldson sped over the country roads.

"The children did look lovely, didn't they? I do not know which was the prettiest," she exclaimed enthusiastically.

"They were certainly very cute and picturesque," replied her companion, smiling at her almost childish delight. "Little May

Cornell was most fetching in 'Comin' through the Rye.' Did you notice how thoroughly the little youngster entered into the spirit of the scene? Her small lover's only regret, I am sure, was that the tableau was so short."

"Well, you know the old adage, 'It is love which makes the world go round,'" and she hummed lightly the air of a merry chanson. It was a beautiful night, warm without being oppressive. The moonlight threw shadows upon the hills, and was reflected in the many brooks as they gurgled by; the lights of various houses twinkled through the trees, looking in the distance as if stars had fallen amid the leaves to lighten the path for wayfarers.

"It is love which makes the world go round in more ways than one," Donald said, with such emphasis that she smiled, amused, yet flushing too. "Love has in some form or another been the inspiration of everything worth having. Even the portraiture of the

human countenance and form was inspired
by love.   You remember, do you not, the interesting character of the Greek maiden,
Cora, whose grief at the enforced separation
from her lover was so overpowering that, beneath its influence of loneliness and despair,
and longing to retain at least some sort of
tangible representation of the one she loved,
she made in bas-relief, on the impulse of the
moment, the image of his form and features
—the first portrait of a human being ever
given to mankind?"

   "Yes, indeed," replied the girl.   "She
was the daughter of Dibutades, was she not?
It is a sweet story; the tenderer because
true.   I have always felt glad that her gift
to the world was rewarded by proving the in-
strument which gave her at last her heart's
desire.   It must be very dreadful to be separated from some one whom one loves so
deeply," she added thoughtfully; then, re-
membering how soon Donald was going
away, she hesitated with sudden shyness.

"Espérance, I am going away—leaving shortly for a long stay. If I could but think, but hope——" he stopped abruptly. Had he not vowed that he would not so much as tell her of his love till he had a future to offer her?

"Hello, where are you two going?" called Dr. Thornsdale. "I declare we have over-taken you, after all; a very fortunate fact, it seems to me, since you two young people are so busy star-gazing that you don't recognize your own gate—just pass it as if it were not staring you full in the face."

Of course there was a general laugh, in which there was nothing for Espérance to do but to join. But she felt shy and uncomfort-able, especially as Anselm for some unac-countable reason looked black as a thunder-cloud; and she was glad to make her escape as quickly as possible to her own room.

Far into the night she lay awake, won-dering, girl-like, what Donald's unspoken words would have been; why he stopped so abruptly; whether or not the sentence would have been ever finished had they not been interrupted at that moment. Somehow she realized as never before how keenly she would miss Donald Thornsdale when he sailed to the far-off land of her own birth, whither she could not follow. The evening, which had been so merry, ended after all in perplexity that was half sweet, half wistful; and the shadow of a parting which would grieve her, stealing upon her, a tear fell unbidden on the pillow as she tried, at length, to sleep.

CHAPTER IX.

THE EVENING BEFORE DONALD SAILS.

THE weeks sped on, but the sentence interrupted the evening of the tableaux was never finished. Donald blamed himself for his weakness. Had he not firmly resolved not to tell her of his love till he had a right to do so?—that she was too young, knew too little of the world, perhaps too little of her own heart, to speak yet, even were his future assured? Yet he could not but feel that his affection was not wholly unreciprocated, and there were times when silence seemed almost a moral impossibility.

The evening before he sailed, in September, was cool and starlit. Mrs. Thornsdale was busy putting the last finishing touches which only a mother can give to the trunks and valise her boy was to take with him,

and Donald himself had been in deep con-
verse with his father in his private study.
By the open window through which the fra-
grance of the wild rose-bushes was stealing,
the myriad of stars twinkling in the cloud-
less heavens, was Anselm, his handsome face
slightly in shadow as he struck the soft notes
of a guitar in accompaniment to some dreamy
aria which Espérance was playing on the
piano, the yellow shade of the lamp throwing
its mellow light on her white gown and dark
hair. It was a pretty scene, and Donaldson
stood for an instant drinking in each detail,
conscious of a sudden keen pang of jealousy.

"Suppose Anselm——" but he dismissed
the thought instantly with a half smile.
"Anselm — how absurd!" he thought.
"Why, he is a mere boy yet, the deeper side
of his character scarcely formed;" and as the
latter rose eagerly from the divan to make
room for him, he felt ashamed of the jealous
fear, however passing.

"Will you sing my favorite, Espérance?"

he asked; and after a scarcely perceptible hesitancy the girl turned to a folio which he specially liked.

"Too sentimental for me," exclaimed Anselm, in mock deprecation. "Au revoir!" and he ran up the light-wood staircase two steps at a time, just as the full sweet notes of the girl's alto voice floated upward.

"Je pense à toi, toujours."

The voice was clear and steady, but there was a tenderness and pathos in it that night which Donald had never heard before. Or was it that the longing of his own heart made him imagine it?

"Je pense à toi, toujours," he repeated gravely. "It will be so with me forever, Espérance. And you—you will not forget me when I am far away?"

Surely he could say at least that much? surely he could not ask less?—but the tone of his voice spoke volumes, the pleading in his face more eloquently than any words.

"Forget you! Never, Donald." That

was all; but each felt that the other's heart
had pledged much in those simple words.
And as they wandered out into the star-lit garden overlooking the river, with its gleaming
lights, he spoke quietly of his future work
and studies, of his hope to win fame and a
home he could call his own; she, of the nobility of his profession in soothing and healing stricken humanity.   And as they reached
the path close to the ivied veranda, he
stooped suddenly and pressed his lips rever-
ently to the pure brow he loved so well.

"God bless and guard you, my Espérance," he murmured, with inexpressible tenderness.   And Anselm, stepping out on the
porch at that moment, drew hastily back,
and was not surprised when later Donald told
him something of his hopes for the future,
begging him to cherish the girl who had entered so strangely into their lives, and not let
her teach too incessantly.   But Anselm was
dimly conscious of a vague unrest and wondered at it.

CHAPTER X.

"Is any city in the world as fascinating as Paris?" Donald asked himself again and again as the first days of his arrival flew by, each one revealing some new charm of the French metropolis which Espérance had so often depicted in glowing colors. Whatever time he could spare from study he spent in exploring the boulevards, the Bois, and the old parts of the city, less beautiful than the more modern portion, but more quaint and filled with historic associations of centuries, tragic and otherwise. Paris is indeed a centre where joy and sadness, virtue and vice, ancient as well as modern records of humanity focus in an extraordinary degree. To a man of Donald's reflective nature the city with its suggestions of the past mingling

69

with the present was full of special interest.
The mass of people moving leisurely about,
as if time were sufficiently generous to allow
opportunity for everything which life can
afford, both of work and amusement, were
studies of human nature very fascinating to
the medical student of the country " where,"
a Frenchman [1] has lately said with much wit,
" it is a wonder that any one can find time
to die."

" A crowd is not company," however, and
"faces but a gallery of pictures," when the
heart is elsewhere, and Donald never realized
so forcibly the truth of the old adage. Often
homesickness seemed to take almost physical
hold of him, so firm and unbending was its
grip; a fact unsuspected by the many fellow-
students among whom he soon became popular in spite of his reserved nature.

Among the students, whose nationality
varied as much as there are countries in
the world, one particularly attracted him.

[1] Paul Bourget.

L'Estrange was his name—Pierre L'Estrange. He was rather looked down upon by some of his young colleagues, as he came from the middle class of the Parisian people, but Donaldson was too broad-minded to let that fact prejudice him.

Pierre possessed the culture which comes from a naturally refined nature—"nature's gentleman" in very truth. His keen intelligence, his wit and kindliness were congenial to Donald. It was he who introduced him to the various places of interest in Paris and had a fund of anecdotes connected with each to amuse his companion, unconscious that the latter answered and laughed often mechanically, his thoughts with the fair girl across the sea whose image never left him.

Ambitious, eager for knowledge and for the ability to relieve humanity which his learning would bring, Espérance had become, notwithstanding, the goal towards which everything tended, but he only mentioned her casually to Pierre, even after he knew him well.

"Are your parents living?" he asked
L'Estrange one evening shortly after their
acquaintance, as, leaving the university
which is situated across the bridge, they
hailed the little sailboat on the Seine and
drifted up the river, the quiet, unceasing flow
of the water with its gay ripple characteristic of the rush amid leisure of the great city
rising upon either side.

"My father died a few years ago," replied
Pierre, a shadow crossing his bright countenance; "but my mother is living, and my
adopted sister—my cousin in reality—Marienette, who has lived with us since her infancy. She is three years younger than I.
That makes her just eighteen. Si!—but I
am growing quite aged. Twenty-one, ready
to demand all the respect due to veritable
manhood!" with an infectious laugh that
reminded Donaldson of Anselm.

"That is just my brother's age. I wish
you knew him; you would be very congenial."

"Well, if he is like the present representative of the Thornsdale family I do not doubt that fact in the least," and the young Frenchman linked his arm through his companion's in the foreign way characteristic of him, a look of sincere admiration lighting his merry eyes, though he spoke banteringly.

"My home is at Versailles, but I shall make my headquarters at Paris when I graduate, after making a tour of the States. Surgery has made wonderful progress in your country, and you know that will be pre-eminently my line of study."

"Somehow, I cannot imagine you slashing and cutting," Donald answered lightly, with a quick, affectionate glance at the boyish, clean-shaven face and laughing blue eyes, suggestive of a schoolboy rather than a surgeon-elect.

Reaching the Champs Elysées they alighted and soon entered the Bois. It was a Saturday afternoon, and, though the last day of September, it was warm and pleasant as a May day. The park presented as gay a scene as in spring. As is usual in Paris, and indeed throughout France, on Saturday and Sunday afternoons, entire families were seen strolling or seated together in groups, the mother beaming with matronly pride and " le père de la famille" enjoying to his utmost his holiday with the little ones—"les petits enfants."

"And yet people say there is no domestic life among the French," mused Donald aloud.

"Who has said that?" asked Pierre in his quick way. "The Americans? I thought they were too just to think of anything so absurd. But, ah! they do not know us, those poor Americans," and the compassion of the last words was so sincere that Donald laughed, amused at the young Frenchman's enthusiasm.

"Look! what is that group descending from that omnibus?" he asked.

"A bridal party," Pierre replied with a shrug. "You know that among the bourgeois it is customary for the bride, immediately after the ceremony, to hold a *fête* in the Bois instead of at home. Bride and groom, parents and grandparents, troop into the park and dance and feast the entire afternoon. See, there is another party yonder. A pretty sight, is it not?" And, indeed, the scene was very picturesque. Under the trees, the sunlight gleaming through the leaves, danced young girls in gay costumes with not ungraceful partners, the bride, clad in white with veil and wreath, in their midst, the older people looking benevolently on and tapping their feet in time to the music.

As Donald watched the groom's attention to his pretty wife of an hour, Heine's description came vividly to him, and he teasingly quoted it to Pierre.

"A Frenchman's love for his bride glows and flames; he throws himself at her feet with the most exaggerated protestations; he fights for her to the death; he will commit a thousand follies for her sake. Is that what you will do, my friend?" he added mischievously.

"Yes, I will do that," answered Pierre with unexpected gravity, "but I will do more. I will prove by my life that I look up to her as the angel of home—the sanctuary of every true man who calls a true woman wife. Home is either heaven or hell, particularly to a Frenchman." Then, as if conscious that he had spoken with unusual warmth, he said with a light laugh: "You remember the old saying, 'There is either heaven or hell for the French, but no purgatory'?"

Chatting merrily they retraced their steps and soon reached their pension, Pierre unsuspicious of the surprise awaiting him. As he opened the entrance door a musical laugh greeted them, and a bewitching little creature, clad in a coquettish gown of brown and blue, darted forward with a low courtesy.

"Je suis bien contente de vous voir, Mon-

sieur," and then almost before Pierre had
time to exclaim "Marienette!" with astonished delight, she threw her arms around his
neck.

"I thought you would be surprised, you
dear darling," then noting Donald's tall form
towering above Pierre, she flushed slightly
and drew back confused.

"Quel grand monsieur!" she thought.

"Will you not introduce me to your sister?" the "grand monsieur" was just saying
with amused courtesy.

"Pardon," said Pierre. "Marienette, this
is my new friend of whom I have already
written—Monsieur Thornsdale. And where
is mother?" as the girl made a slight bow
with much grace to the stranger.

"She will be with us in a few moments.
Not finding you at home, Maman went to
purchase some articles at the shop near by.
Ah! here she comes now," and Donald, feeling that his presence would be a constraint,
left them with a murmured excuse.

" An attractive child," he thought. " She would amuse mother," and in a few moments forgot all about her as he commenced a long letter to Anselm full of amusing incidents.

CHAPTER XI.

BEFORE another year glided by, a change full of sadness passed over Espérance's new home. Death, crossing its threshold, robbed her of the kind friend who had been like a father to her. The strong, kindly man, whose cheery voice and big heart had carried sunshine and healing to so many anxious homes, after a brief illness succumbed to the spectre whose grip upon others he had so often relaxed. An epidemic prevalent in the city during the preceding winter attacking him, pneumonia quickly set in, and within a few days he passed away, leaving a void and loneliness indescribable in the loving hearts left to struggle still on the battlefield of life, upon which he had served with honor until the end.

79

What Mrs. Thornsdale would have done without Espérance during those trying days and the dreary weeks and months which followed, she often said she could not even imagine. The girl's unfailing, unobtrusive sympathy, her courage in spite of her own heart being sorely grieved, was a source of consolation and help to the bereaved wife which she alone could fully appreciate. Less than ever could she part with Espérance, who, true to her name, breathed a spirit of hope and tender comfort throughout even that saddened home.

The girl herself would have been loath to leave, and indeed she felt no longer free to do so even had she desired it. Dr. Thornsdale, realizing his condition, made Espérance promise that she would never leave his wife unless it were in case of her own marriage, and begged Mrs. Thornsdale not to let his death disturb in any way Donald's study and work abroad. "You will have Anselm and Espérance also with you, my wife, at least till Donaldson returns.   Were he with me, I would beg him to promise me not to alter his plans and thus spoil his future career.   When he comes back for good, he will be fully competent to fill my position; but see that he finishes his course there—it is my—earnest —request—my——," but he had been unable to speak further, losing consciousness soon after and regaining it only for a brief space just at the last.   He died in his faithful wife's arms, the stillness broken only by the voice of Espérance as she read the beautiful prayers for the dying.

Donald returned at once for a few weeks, remaining just long enough to arrange some business matters with Anselm.   In compliance with his father's dying wish, he returned to Paris, though dreading the second separation from his mother and Espérance.   The latter he had scarcely seen, except with others, during his sad visit home.

The following summer " Lalla Rookh," their country-seat, was rented, and Mrs.

6

Thornsdale travelled with Espérance, Anselm
joining them each evening, when they were
within possible reach of the city.   His apparent devotion to his mother, his consideration for herself, touched Espérance.   It
never occurred to her that it was any actual desire to be with her individually,
which accounted in great part for his arrival at times and places when least expected.   Unconsciously, perhaps, even to
himself, Anselm had become more and
more dependent upon her companionship.
He scarcely realized how completely he had
fallen beneath the spell of her thousand winning ways, her rare beauty, her quick sympathy in all that concerned him.   Donald's
confidence the evening before he sailed for
Europe, instead of warning him against becoming too interested in her, made him less
suspicious of the possible danger of falling
in love with her himself.   From that night
he was quite persuaded that he looked upon
her only in the light of a future sister, for

he guessed that Donald's affection was far
from being unreciprocated. Surely, however,
though subtly, he became more and more devoted to her. It was when circumstances
separated them for several consecutive weeks
that the realization of how utterly blank his
daily life was without her came upon him
with the suddenness of a shock. But Anselm's nature was not such as to relinquish
readily, much less gracefully, to another anything he desired. Even in childhood that
trait of character was visible, often troubling
both his parents, generous-hearted in every.
way themselves; but the mother felt sure as
the boy grew older that he had outgrown any
latent actual selfishness or meanness of character. Instead of flying temptation, Anselm
tried to persuade himself, as days passed on,
that Donald's affection for Espérance was
but a passing infatuation after all, which
doubtless in the practical life of hard study
and work of all these months had ceased even
to exist. He certainly did not write her

with any marked frequency, nor did he speak a great deal of her, even in his letters to him, which would be but natural after their conversation the evening before he sailed. Yet that very silence should have told him how deep was the love his brother bore her, for he knew well that Donald's natural reserve made him the more reticent when keenly affected.

CHAPTER XII.

ONE Sunday morning, shortly after their return to the city, Anselm, settling himself in an easy-chair, cigarette in hand, began to glance lazily over the columns of the *Herald*. Suddenly he started forward with an exclamation of surprise.

"Thornsdale — L'Estrange. In Paris, Wednesday, August 31st, at the English Chapel, Rue d'Alma, by the Rev. Jonathan Platt, Donaldson Thurston Thornsdale to Marienette L'Estrange."

"Impossible, impossible!" he muttered with suppressed excitement. "What can it mean?" and even as he exclaimed, his glance fell upon a notice at the bottom of the page: "The announcement of the marriage of

85

Donaldson Thurston Thornsdale to Marienette L'Estrange, which was privately solem-
nized at the English Chapel in the Rue
d'Alma over five weeks ago, has created quite
a furore in the professional circles of which
the groom was the centre. The fact that the
wedding has been kept secret has given rise
to various surmises. The bride is young,
pretty in appearance, and refined, but as she
comes from the lower ranks of life the marriage is regarded as a mésalliance, which pos-
sibly accounts for Thornsdale's wish (if re-
port be true) that the union should be kept
secret. If the rumor is correct, the announcement of his marriage, therefore, may
not be altogether welcome to the newly made
benedict, whose career promised to be one of
unusual brilliancy, and who, it is said, in spite
of a certain reserve of manner, is the most
popular man of his class."

"Are you there, Anselm?" It was Espérance's voice, and he started involuntarily.
What would she, Espérance, think of these

notices? Had he better show them to her, or wait?

"Your mother is asking for the papers," she said, pushing the door wide open. "Have you finished with them?"

"Yes — no—that is—here are some of them," he said abruptly.

"But it is the *Herald* she particularly wants, on account of the Paris news, you know."

"I understand," he replied quickly; "but the fact is—there," with sudden determination. "Read that and see what you can make of it."

It was cruel to give her no preparation. In a glance she grasped the significance of the announcement. She turned deathly pale and for a second said nothing. It was as if she had received a sudden blow. But quickly regaining her self-possession, she threw the paper aside.

"It is a mistake, of course," she said with a shrug of her shoulders. "Of course, it cannot be Donald," but her voice trembled slightly, and Anselm, noting its unsteadiness and the pallor of the beautiful face that haunted him night and day, hardened as if he were stone.

"It is strange, very strange," he answered. "The name is uncommon, and even the middle one is the same; his characteristic reserve is mentioned, his very career implied. Nothing is wanting. Mother must not see this paper."

"Do you believe this to be true?" she asked, a ring of defiance in her voice.

"I believe it refers to my brother, certainly," he answered with decision, though evasively. "There are clearly not two Donaldson Thurston Thornsdales in the world. We must wait till we hear from Donaldson himself."

"Have you no relatives of a similar name?"

"No. My father had no brother or even sister. The only relatives he had were distant, and their name was not the same."

"What will you do about keeping the journal from Mrs. Thornsdale? Oh, it is absurd, absurd!" she exclaimed, clasping her hands with the unconscious mannerism which betrayed her foreign blood whenever excited or earnest. "It is impossible that Donald could have married unknown to us all. Your mother would know that at once. You cannot believe she would be misled by the notice," and she flushed with indignant scorn, angry at herself for having been even passingly disconcerted. But Anselm was determined. He answered cautiously, however:

"It will of course be explained sooner or later, Espérance; but in the meanwhile I must insist that mother shall be kept in ignorance of these announcements."

"Why, there is but one!" she exclaimed, startled.

For answer, Anselm pointed to the second detailed notice at the bottom of the page, and again she paled, and this time her hand was not quite steady.

"It must be as you wish, of course," she said in a peculiar voice as she turned to leave the room, the remaining papers in her hand. "What excuse shall I make for not bringing the *Herald?*"

"Tell mother I will be up in a moment. Do not worry. Leave it to me. I will concoct some excuse or other."

"Oh, I would not think of usurping a lawyer's privilege. The unravelling of difficulties is a lawyer's exclusive province."

She spoke with a light laugh, with that sudden transition from seriousness to badinage which to him was so fascinating even when it puzzled him; but her face was very white as she went slowly up-stairs, and her words had a ring which made him feel vaguely uncomfortable.

CHAPTER XIII.

SUSPENSE.

DAYS passed, and Espérance tried to persuade herself that the marriage announcements which had so startled Anselm and herself were the outcome of some unfortunate mistake. "It cannot, simply cannot, be Donald," she repeated again and again to herself; but do what she would, she could not still the unrest which filled her. It was scarcely credible that two men should, without any connecting link of relationship, bear a similar uncommon name, follow the same career, possess even a similar characteristic of manner. That a marriage between a Donaldson Thurston Thornsdale to a certain Marienette L'Estrange did actually occur upon a certain date in Paris there could be no doubt. The only question to be solved

91

was, who was this particular Donaldson
Thornsdale? With feverish impatience she
awaited the usual home letters of Donald.
He must have seen the marriage notices in
the Paris edition of the paper, she reasoned,
and would comment upon them if only as a
joke. But though the mail, with one or two
exceptions, came with the usual regularity,
no light was thrown in any way upon the
subject, which, in spite of herself, was troubling her more and more. Mrs. Thornsdale,
with happy unsuspiciousness and with all a
mother's pride, would read aloud to Espérance the epistles always full of interesting
incidents, amusing and otherwise. Had the
mother been less engrossed, she must have
suspected something from the tell-tale color
which would come and go in the tender,
mobile face beside her, bent low over some
piece of embroidery or—which was far more
likely—over some garment for the poor.
Were it true, how cruelly he was deceiving
the mother who loved him so ardently, she

would think involuntarily—how superficial must have been his affection for herself.

" An affection which could so quickly be transferred to another would not be worth winning," she would murmur proudly. Perhaps she might even have misunderstood the thousand little signs which seemed at the time to be clearest evidence that she was all in all to him; but as the thought suggested itself she would flush with humiliation, the keener because conscious of the sharp pain in her heart at the mere possibility of his faithlessness. " No one shall know how it hurts—ah, how it hurts!" she would add piteously. And then the noble, strong face of the man who loved her would rise before her as if to rebuke her doubting, and she would cry out that it was impossible that he, her true, honest-hearted Donald, could be disloyal, that she could have been so deceived.

Yet, after all, he was free to marry. He was not bound to her in any way. And

immediately, woman-like, she would begin
to wonder what this Marienette L'Estrange
looked like—was she tall or short, blonde or
brunette, gay or—and then would interrupt
the thought with a feeling of indignation
against her own stupidity and credulity.

If he would write, were it only one word,
to throw some light upon it all. The suspense was growing intolerable. Anselm,
watching her closely, saw she was becoming
more and more troubled, and the knowledge
filled him with a certain though as yet half-
defined feeling of triumph. Did she become
fully convinced that Donald had been disloyal to her and had actually married, would
there not be some chance for him—Anselm
—gradually to win her? Were he at last to
succeed, how happy, ah, how happy, he would
make her. The thought was delirium. She
would without doubt learn to forget the man
who had so easily and quickly forgotten her.
But Anselm Thornsdale knew he was lying
to his own conscience when he thus reasoned.

That there was some mistake he did not actually doubt an instant; yet he tried to believe the announcements, and thus quiet the
"still, small voice" which warned him that
he was acting treacherously in emphasizing
upon a mere uncertainty to the woman his
brother loved, every possible point of evidence against him, and in not notifying him
at once of the announcements and their own
perplexity as to who this Donald Thornsdale
could be. "Time enough, time enough yet
to let him know," he would say to himself,
and then wonder what action Espérance
would decide upon, or whether she had cared
as much as he had thought for Donaldson.

Yes, Espérance had cared much for
Donald, but it was the dawning rather than
the completion of love. She was inexperi-
enced in the ways of the world; and the
memory of her mother's years of suffering,
caused by the faithlessness of the husband
to whose affection and nobility of character
she had blindly confided, was too fresh to

fail as a warning against trusting too completely, too keen not to make her shrink at
the barest possibility of her own heart-affec-
tion and confidence being rejected and mis-
placed.

"Anselm," she said one evening, unable
to bear the suspense any longer, joining him
while he was writing in the library, " I have
been thinking about it, and I am convinced
you ought to notify your—your brother about
those articles in the paper. Can you not
enclose them in your letter to-night?"

"Why, yes, I can do so certainly," he replied, not knowing well how to refuse, and
somewhat taken aback by her sudden acknowledgment that the subject had troubled
her.

" Did you keep that particular edition of
the paper?" she asked.

" I cut the articles out."

"Both?" she asked a little hesitatingly.

Somehow her timidity, the eager, unconscious pleading in her young face, touched

him that night. Poor child, she already had
had much sorrow in her short life. For the
time his better nature was roused. Opening
a secret drawer of his desk he took out the
articles and placed them in the unsealed letter lying there.

"Are you not going to add a few words of
explanation?" she inquired, surprised.

"Of course. How stupid of me!" and
jotting a few hasty lines by way of postscript,
he said something about catching the nine
o'clock mail, and hurried out as if not daring
to tarry; and Espérance with a half-sob threw
herself into the low arm-chair beside the fire,
which crackled merrily as if to cheer as well
as warm her.

Anselm reached the mail-box just as the
town clock struck nine.

"Too late for to-night, I guess," he muttered, and for an instant he stood irresolute.
Were he not to mail it after all what consequences would follow? Donald, unconscious
of the announcements, would of course make

7

no response, and Espérance, thinking Anselm
had forwarded them, could but interpret his
silence in one way. Was it not the consciousness that silence was against Donald
which had made him delay sending the clippings of his own accord?   Yet, as the thought
of delaying the letter for that one reason took
definite shape, he flushed scarlet, and murmuring, " No, I cannot be quite as despicable as
that; he must at least have this one chance,"
he quickly opened the box to drop the letter
in, not noting in his haste that, instead of
falling into the mail-box, it fluttered to the
ground.

CHAPTER XIV.

A BUTTERFLY.

In a dainty cottage, low-roofed and ivy-covered, not far from "Le Petit Trianon," a very young girl flitted to and fro as pretty and gay as a butterfly, arranging flowers first in one vase then in another, in the small drawing-room overlooking the garden.

Stopping in front of a long mirror, she gazed critically at the reflection in the narrow glass. That she was conscious of the charm it revealed was easy to suspect from the pleased smile that lighted the gray-blue eyes with coquetry.

"Yes, you will do, Mademoiselle Marie-nette. You are quite presentable in every way, though your nose will turn up most provokingly. But if he does not care, why should you?" with a little sigh of contentment.

116250B

"I do wish Maman and Pierre knew, but they would never have consented while I am so young," and she stepped from the long French window to the porch near which a deer was grazing on the smooth grass.

She could see the woods where the youthful wife of Louis XVI. loved to roam and cast aside, at least for a while, the trammels of court etiquette, so irksome to her gay nature. She could catch a glimpse through the trees of the little "Trianon," where the girl-queen became for the nonce a simple dairy-maid, churning the milk and cream. There was something sympathetic to her in the waywardness of the girlish queen, and her sad fate appealed to her in all its pathos. Much unsuspected depth slumbered in her own untamed nature, waiting for some unknown touch to awaken it.

All at once her face brightened with a comical expression of mingled fright and mischief.

"There is Maman! What shall I do? Fate is against us!"

"How pretty the flowers are, chérie," said Madame L'Estrange, as she entered the drawing-room a moment later. "I received a telegram from Pierre, and he will be here in the six o'clock train, perhaps earlier, and it is after four now. I should not be surprised if Monsieur Thornsdale accompanied him." She did not note the somewhat startled expression of Marienette.

"I would not be at all astonished if Monsieur Thornsdale were here this evening," was the demure reply. "Oh, it is a shame to deceive so good a mother," she thought with quick compunction.

"Let me remove your bonnet, dearest," she said with unusual gentleness; "and then you must lie down on the couch and rest until Pierre comes." And the elder woman, humoring her, let her do as she wished.

Ten minutes later, Marienette hastened to the garden gate and stood gazing down the road with anxious eyes. She had not long to wait, and spying a tall, familiar figure sauntering towards her, she almost flew through the gateway.

"You must not come. Maman is home and Pierre is expected. Hark! There are wheels now!" Her pretty face flushed with excitement, and they had just time to conceal themselves behind some large bushes when a cab passed them.

"It is Pierre——" but the man interrupted her with a peculiar laugh.

"Well, what of it? They must know sooner or later—why not at once?"

"Because they must not," with an impatient stamp of the small foot. "Quick, let me go and I will meet you here an hour later," and, like a veritable butterfly in her yellow gown,.she flitted past him, reaching the cottage almost as soon as Pierre.

CHAPTER XV.

THE TWO LETTERS.

"A LETTER for Anselm, and one for me," Mrs. Thornsdale said, entering the breakfast-room a few weeks after Anselm had forwarded the articles to Donald.. "Dinah brought them to my room as soon as the mail came. The name of the student he finds so charming," she continued, pouring the coffee, "is L'Estrange—Pierre L'Estrange. He says he has had rather a struggle in life. His mother and his young cousin, who has been like a sister to him—what is her name—Mari-—Marienette, a pretty——" but Espérance stayed not to hear. With a murmured excuse she left the table, not daring to trust herself to remain, and meeting Anselm just as he entered the dining-room. Scarcely returning his salutation, she fled upstairs, leaving him for a moment a little bewildered.

"Is Espérance not well, mother?" he asked, surprised and somewhat anxious.

"Oh, yes, I think she just forgot something, or it may be a passing indisposition. We have letters from Don again to-day," she said, handing him his. "Or here is mine first, if you wish."

Anselm scanned the letter leisurely, but as his eye fell upon the clause referring to Pierre L'Estrange, he scarcely repressed an exclamation. Espérance's hurried departure from the table was more than explained. What further proof was needed? The marriage announcements, now that they had received Donald's own acknowledgment of his new friend's name and of the existence of his adopted sister, Marienette L'Estrange, combined with the fact that Donald had spoken of this same student as a man of unusual mental calibre, though not possessing a high social position, were no longer difficult to fathom. For the first time Anselm actually believed that his brother, blinded by sudden passion, had married beneath him, and the realization that his conviction was now sincere brought with it a sense of relief from strain, relief from the ceaseless pricking of conscience that he was not treating Donald fairly. It was characteristic of his absorption in self that he did not think of his mother's eventual suffering when the knowledge came to her, as it sooner or later must. His one thought was Espérance. She now could doubt no longer. He was free, perfectly free to win her. That he would succeed in those first moments he did not doubt. He was in a gale of spirits all through breakfast, the black, boldly written lines of that other missive lying close at his hand.

CHAPTER XVI.

MAY, always so fair a month in Paris, seemed doubly bright that spring. Each tree was a fairy-like bower, pink and green and white, the varied blossoms scenting the air with delicious perfume and making the city a vast garden of enchanting beauty.

Early one evening the two friends strolled through the Champs Elysées, the colored lights of the cafés chantants glimmering through the foliage, and strains of music floating outwards as if to entice the passers-by to enter the luring precincts, if only for a while. Certainly there is no city in the world where evil dons a more bewitching garb than Paris.

Retracing their steps, Pierre and Donaldson sauntered down the boulevards, bright

with light and life, as if it were midday,
and sat down at an outside table of the café
at the corner of the Rue de Rivoli. With
lazy interest they watched the motley crowd
passing to and fro, Pierre now and then
making remarks upon individual peculiarities
with the keen French wit which, however
sparkling, is seldom unkind.

Suddenly the graceful form of a young girl
hastened past, the reflection of the street
lamp revealing a pale yet far from unattrac-
tive face, with blue eyes that just then had
a pained, startled look like one suddenly
wounded. A few feet back of her were a
man and woman, the latter rather conspicu-
ously dressed and evidently amused, the
former annoyed yet haughty.

To Thornsdale's surprise, Pierre hurried
forward, and in another instant was greeting
the young girl, whose face lighted with welcome, then clouded again.

"Not now, Monsieur L'Estrange; I cannot explain. It all happened a short while

ago. . . My unfortunate mother. . . We are stopping at the hotel — not far from here——"

The broken words Donald could not quite catch, but he heard another voice distinctly.

"Oh, Monsieur, how glad I am to see you. Where did you drop from? My step-daughter will be more than pleased," with a little affected laugh, "and my husband you already know." Pierre gave the gayly dressed owner of the rather loud voice a freezing glance and bowed slightly.

"Your husband, Madame," he said with marked sarcasm, "I have had the pleasure of knowing a long while. Mademoiselle, I shall have the honor of calling soon." And pressing the girl's cold hand, held instinctively out to him, he rejoined his astonished friend.

"That is Mademoiselle Charbon, of whom you have heard me speak," he said, his face flushed with the excitement of the unexpected meeting. "That was her father with the divorcée whom he married a short while ago."

"And is his first wife dead?" asked Donald curiously.

"Dead? No; she ran off with another man."

"He had some excuse then, had he not? I feel rather sorry for him." And Donald looked for an instant amused.

"Excuse! Yes, in a way. That is why, I suppose, Mademoiselle chose to stay with the father, since one parent she had to remain with. But," he hastened to add, "in reality he had no excuse—no real moral excuse. Two evils do not make one right."

"Of course not," answered Donald decidedly.

"*Tiens!* there he is now," and Pierre leaned eagerly forward. "Do you see that short but rather good-looking man crossing the boulevard? That is the man her mother ran away with. They must have passed him before they passed here, and that accounts for poor little Mam'selle's startled expression. She is a sensitive, high-minded girl and feels deeply humiliated about these separations. Her mother I met in the Bois only yesterday. I should think they would have the decency to remain at least in different cities. It is a comparatively short while since the French Government with all its faults sanctioned by law this polite bigamy; this convenient exchange of husbands or wives, as the case may be. It makes a Frenchman with a drop of loyal blood in his veins blush for his country. It is the natural complement of the dethronement of the highest type of womanhood a century ago from the pedestals of France for the installation of a pagan deity, the protectress of vice."

"Divorce is certainly a terrible evil and a widespreading one," said Donald. "In America, between 1866 and 1885, there were five hundred thousand applications for divorce,

so the official census tells us, and since then
the number has been still greater."

"The States, then, need to take warning
as well as France, for divorce is nothing less
than the upheaval of society. A light regard of the marriage tie, degrading wifehood
and motherhood, saps the national life, leading it to destruction, as we can see from
Greece, Rome, and other nations of ancient
fame."

"The highest civilization has been founded
on monogamy, without doubt," replied
Donald. "It is the family that forms the
state."

"Exactly. 'Give me good mothers,' said
Napoleon, 'and I will give you good citi-
zens.' "

"Bony hit the nail on the head that time,"
said Donald with a smile.

"Yes, indeed. But if marriage is reduced
to the level of a mere business transaction,
his country will not have heeded his words
any more than the world at large. Divorce,

desecrating home, inevitably lowers woman and deprives the offspring of at least one natural protector. To eject Christianity out of laws is to crush purest civilization."

"Yes; even the infidel Proudhon asserts that 'theology (Christianity) is at the bottom of our laws,' yet it seems hard, after all, that an innocent wife, for example, should remain tied to a brute as one does see sometimes," replied Donald thoughtfully.

"True, but for one case of such unhappiness there will be hundreds of far greater misery if the marriage bond is lightly regarded. The evil will be intensified in proportion as restraint is lessened. Persons will enter the married state with far graver consideration if they realize the step is sacred and irrevocable; will guard more imperatively against mistake if they know there is no loophole for escape. An unhappy marriage, dreadful misfortune though it is, must be endured, as are other sorrows of great magnitude."

"Right again, my sage philosopher; yet I imagine that very good persons believe conscientiously in divorce."

"Without doubt.   But it is difficult to see how any Christian could marry a divorced person without qualm of conscience.   For a Catholic, it would be an impossibility."

"I wonder if our prehistoric ancestors gave and were given in marriage?" asked Donald mischievously.

"Well, if our respective ancestors were of the ape genus, I fear we will look in vain to them for help in problems of morality.   I cannot say that I should feel honored or elevated by such ancestry," added Pierre with a light laugh; "as for the prehistoric man, seriously speaking, I question much his existence."

"The fossil remains in the quaternary formations of the globe may have something to say about that," said Donald dryly.

"The famous Moulin-Quignon jaw-bone, particularly," was the malicious reply.   "Poor

8

Monsieur de Berthes! How discomfited he must have been at the discovery that the fossils for which he offered so high a reward were but ordinary human bones dug up from a graveyard of the victims of the fourteenth-century plague, and transferred to another spot to hoodwink poor, unsuspecting gentlemen—too wise to accept anything except the evidence of their senses!"

Donaldson laughed good-humoredly.

"Those workmen were clever devils. The way they arranged that de Berthes should be present at the digging up, after leaving the bones in their new ground for months, was too neat a plan to end in failure. And it certainly did succeed, at first admirably, for both French and English geologists believed them to be genuine old fossils of prehistoric times."

"Shortly before Romulus founded Rome, the Tiber, you know," said Pierre, "had not yet ceased to be in the condition requisite for quaternary formations, such as the strata in which fossil remains of man have been actually found, and which formed, beyond doubt, when the water-courses were of far greater extent than now. Why other rivers with such formations should point to a higher antiquity, I cannot see."

"Well, in any case, scientists disagree to a large extent about these strata, and all admit that little has been ascertained about them."

"And yet we Catholics are unprogressive because we still maintain that man did not exist anterior to the time given in the Mosaic record!"

They had wended their way homeward during the discussion, and in crossing the bridge they paused a moment to watch the water flowing quietly on, with the lights of the city reflected in it. Donald thought of the flow of human life that never ceases, yet is ebbing more and more surely into the ocean of infinity, and it oppressed him; but the stars in the clear firmament above seemed

to rebuke him and speak of a master hand
mighty enough to unravel the deepest mys-
teries.

> "All nature is but art unknown to thee ;
>   All chance, direction, which thou canst not see ;
>   All discord, harmony not understood ;
>   All partial evil, universal good."
>   —*Pope.*

CHAPTER XVII.

ANSELM, hurrying to meet an appointment, and overrun all the morning with impatient clients, did not open Donald's letter to himself till late in the afternoon. Alone in his office, the crackling of the grate fire was the only sound to disturb the silence. He hastily tore the envelope, two pieces of paper fluttering to the ground.

PARIS, May 12th.

DEAR ANSELM:

As you doubtless have surmised, my life has been of more or less even tenor; but a rather extraordinary coincidence broke for a while its prosaic routine in a way which bade fair to be not altogether pleasant in spite of its comic side. Do you remember hearing father speak of a distant relative by the name of *Thurston Thornsdale Donaldson*

117

(my own name reversed, please notice)? He was third cousin to father, who at one time saw much of him, becoming so attached to him that he named me Donaldson after him, the Thurston being, as you know, an old family name coming down from some remote ancestor. Well, it appears that this Thurston Donaldson (whose namesake I am) made a most unfortunate marriage, and going to India to live, father lost track of him many years ago, for his letters to him were never answered. Whether they ever reached him, he never knew. To make a long story short, the son of this Thurston Thornsdale Donaldson came to Paris to study art, for which he has marked talent; a brilliant man, I fancy, but unscrupulous and erratic. By way of concealing to a certain extent his identity, and partly no doubt through freak, he took the liberty of reversing his name, and is known in the art circles of Paris by the very same name as your humble servant, *Donaldson Thurston Thornsdale.* The enclosed clippings were shown me one day after the class had adjourned by no less a personage than the president of the college, a clever

man, but brusk and without over-much faith
in human nature. He had come across
the marriage notices in overlooking some
back numbers of the *Herald*. Imagine my
amazement—doubled by the fact that the
bride in question bore the precise and very
odd name of my chum's adopted sister, Marienette L'Estrange. Puzzled by the double
coincidence, I had recourse at once to Pierre.
That very evening he received a heart-broken
letter from his mother telling him of the
elopement of Marienette with an art student,
Donaldson Thurston Thornsdale. The young
benedict had better beware. He has done
an extraordinary as well as an illegal thing.
L'Estrange is indignant and awfully upset by
the whole matter, and if only for his sake, I
will make no public protest. After all, what
matters it to me if another man usurps my
name, even unlawfully, provided I am not
held to account for his erratic peccadilloes.
My bachelorhood firmly re-established, I can
afford to laugh, though it might have proved
anything but a laughing matter even for me.
Had the announcements appeared in the
American edition of the paper, my friends

on the other side of the Atlantic might have
been unpleasantly startled. Truly, truth is
stranger than fiction. Mother and Espérance
will be amused and enjoy the whole thing as
a good joke.   In haste,

DONALD.

Without a pause Anselm read the fatal
letter straight to the end, mechanically stooping to pick up the clippings fluttering in the
air. Donaldson was free—free to win, as
he assuredly would, the prize he, Anselm,
coveted so passionately.

The beautiful face with its ever-varying
expression, the thousand winning ways, rose
before his mental vision as if to taunt him.

"It shall not be; I cannot, will not,
give her up," he whispered, a look like
that of a hunted animal crossing his white
face. But how prevent it? Why, destroy
the letter, of course. Very simple. She
would never suspect. Then something else
rose before him—the memory of Donald's
own tenderness for him since childhood;

but it caused an irresoluteness so slight that it could scarcely be called hesitation. He threw back his head with a short, unmirthful laugh.

" A slip of paper will not balk me quite so easily—quite—so—easily!" And he deliberately threw the letter into the heart of the fire, which, blazing up, threw crimson shadows upon his ashen face, even as the treacherous act branded his soul with the scarlet stain of a Judas-sin.

CHAPTER XVIII.

TRANSITION.

THAT deliberate act of treachery seemed to be the final death-knell of conscience. From that time on, it was as if that interior monitor were, in truth, dead beyond hope of resurrection. Anselm was possessed of but one idea, one aspiration—the winning of Espérance. Well he knew that the blow to the girl's heart and pride had been deep, that it would be useless to give then any outward evidence of the passion consuming him. His love must conquer at last—he could afford to wait. Donald had been away not quite two years, and it would be as long, perhaps longer, before his studies and his training in the hospitals abroad would be ended. Reasoning thus, he bided his time, and gradually his unwavering devotion won its victory.

Another year passed by. Espérance still
thought of Anselm in the simple affectionate way as of old — the "dear boy," she
used to call him with the tenderness of a
matron of ninety. But suddenly the "dear
boy" lost much of the boyishness which often
had been irksome even while it amused her.
He was far graver than of old; at times
preoccupied and silent. At first she attributed the change to the responsibilities of a
professional career and to the increasing dependence of his mother upon him since his
father's death, the greater because of the
absence of the other son. But gradually she
learned to see and interpret rightly his unceasing devotion to herself—Espérance Le
Clerque—who felt she could give him in
return only a sister's affection. Anselm
understood and waited. Slowly but surely,
his ardent love, his unceasing consideration
for her, together with his apparent tender
care of his mother, made her think she had
done injustice to his force and depth of

character. Little by little, step by step, she grew to esteem and care for him in a way different from before. A feeling of shyness crept over her whenever with him, and she knew he would not keep silence much longer. Yet she hesitated. Something told her she could never give him the full strength of affection she could have given Donald had he proved all that she had believed him to be, and an impatient sigh that was half regret would break from her. Well, whatever she might have felt was past all possibility of ever reviving. Indignation, contempt for his continued deceit towards the mother who so loved him, grew stronger and stronger as time went on. She had ceased long ago to doubt the existence of his marriage. The links of evidence had to her seemed too connected to be aught else but convincing, strengthened as they partly were by little details clear enough to understand when the riddle was once solved, but which then appeared like so many more in the chain of evidence against him.

More than once she was impelled to write to Donald herself, but she feared he might interpret it in a way the mere thought of which brought the color to her cheeks. Never, never should he have the slightest opportunity of thinking she cared ever so slightly. And thus pride kept her from writing the letter which would have caused everything to be explained; from alluding in any way in the letters which for form's sake and to guard Mrs. Thornsdale from all suspicion, she still wrote him, to her knowledge of that mysterious wedding in the little English chapel at Paris. Poor Donald! Poor Espérance! how little either suspected the scheme which one they loved and trusted was first indirectly, then directly, weaving about them.

CHAPTER XIX.

AN EVENTFUL SHOWER.

"Is Miss Espérance at home, Dinah?" asked Anselm one sultry afternoon towards the last of July, as the negress was polishing the door opening on the ivy-covered porch.

"You'll find her in the garden, I reckon, Massa Anselm; she and them flowers are kinder wedded, I guess," and Dinah shook her close-cropped head, grinning at her own joke.

"Here I am, Anselm," said Espérance, emerging from a cosy nook on the piazza, novel in hand. "Too warm a day to read anything deep," she said, pointing to the book she had been reading.

"'A Question of Honor,'" read Anselm aloud. "That sounds as though it might be deep," and he handed back the book rather

hurriedly, his face flushing, though his words
sounded careless enough.

"It is cool, driving; what do you say to a
drive to the Point?   I have the phaeton here;
come just as you are; any change would be
for the worse," he said mockingly; but the
girl blushed beneath the admiration in his
eyes as he looked down at the winning face
beneath the wide-brimmed hat with its wealth
of wild flowers, a muslin gown of lilac clinging in graceful folds to her slender figure.

"Very well," she answered lightly; "for
better, for worse, as you will," in her confu-
sion stumbling upon words embarrassingly
suggestive, for she did not feel at ease with
him.

"For better, for worse," repeated the man
musingly.   "What would you do were you
to marry and then find it was for the worse?"
he asked with intense earnestness, as they
drove away.

"Be faithful to my promises, of course,
Monsieur," was the prompt reply, though

said in a bantering way; for she feared the turn their conversation had taken, and blamed her own stupidity. " Look! We can see the cadets drilling quite distinctly from this slope. What a beautiful sight!"

Over the undulating hills and green fields with their long grasses blowing gently in the light breeze, the little brooks rushing merrily along here and there, could be seen the gay uniforms glittering in the sunlight, the commanding voice of the colonel echoing over the hill-tops.

" I have often thought there must be soldier blood in my veins. I so love everything pertaining to military life."

" My mother's father was a colonel during the trouble of '65," replied Anselm. " That was a terrible war; it ruined the fortunes and broke up the homes of so many hundreds of worthy people."

" True; but the cause was deserving of limitless sacrifice. Rarely has there been a war fought for a nobler purpose, and the way

the North and South were reconciled, bury-
ing at least all bitterness, was a lesson to
the world. I admire the American people
greatly. Hark! is that thunder, or only the
rumbling of the cannon?"

"Thunder," was the positive answer.
"We must take a short cut home; Dasher
is not any too fond of lightning," turning
the horse's head, who was already pricking
his ears, as a flash opened the heavens.
Quickly they sped along, Espérance chatting
gayly, Anselm watching somewhat anxiously
the black clouds, which grew momentarily
more threatening.

"We will scarcely escape it," he said half
aloud. "Be quiet, Dasher, quiet." But a
tremendous peal of thunder, shaking, it
seemed, the very road beneath them, followed
by a sheet of vivid white light, caused the
horse to start so violently that Espérance,
unprepared for the sudden jerk of the
phaeton, was thrown to the ground. Reck-
less of everything, Anselm jumped from the

9

low carriage, and in a moment was kneeling
beside the unconscious form of the girl, im-
ploring her to speak to him, uttering words
of passionate devotion which the moaning
of the elements seemed to mock.   In that
first minute he feared she was killed.   But
Espérance was not killed.   More stunned
than even wholly unconscious, the dark eyes
opened after an instant that seemed eternity
to him.   She tried to speak but could not;
yet it was not so much faintness which rendered speech impossible just then as the
anguish in the face bent in despairing tenderness over her.

"Thank God!" broke from the man involuntarily.

"It is nothing.   I am not much hurt.
Were you very much frightened, dear?   See,
I can stand; help me."

The endearing epithet escaped her unconsciously in her pity for his pain.

"Are you sure?" he said, as he helped
her with great gentleness to rise.   "My

darling, I thought you were killed," he muttered beneath his breath, as though the mere possibility were too dreadful to utter aloud.

"And you would have been sorry, mon ami?" she asked with an arch little look, a slight quiver in her voice.

"Sorry! Why, even in that one fearful instant it seemed as if life had become a blank. Life has but one meaning, one hope, one aspiration for me—you, Espérance. Oh, my darling," he murmured, regardless of the rain, of everything. "Will you not make me live? You must surely understand," and Anselm, looking into the sweet, drooping face so dear to him, knew that she indeed understood. What mattered the pelting rain, the low rumbling still lingering in the air? What mattered even the fate of poor Dasher —the fate of a loyal heart across the sea? She, for whom he had striven, wooed, sinned, was his at last.

CHAPTER XX.

IT was early in June, the eve of the annual commencement, and within the University all was bustle and excitement.

Preparations on a large scale were being made. The great salon where the diplomas were to be awarded, and the corridors, were graced with flags of the different nations, in honor of the graduates' respective countries, and over the main entrance was draped the flag of France, the fleur-de-lis in white and gold intertwined in the centre.

Never, L'Estrange thought, had he seen his friend more radiant.

For months previous Donald had appeared anxious and often unlike himself, but Pierre at first had attributed it to the approaching trial of the final studies.

"Yet Thornsdale can have no fear as to the result of his examinations," he mused; "something else must be the cause—if you are not in love, my friend, I am very much mistaken," thought the shrewd Frenchman. "I know the symptoms," he would add sentimentally, but with such gravity that the subject of his silent apostrophe would have been amused.

Donald had, in fact, been perplexed and worried as letters from Espérance became less and less frequent. He fancied too that there was an increasing constraint about them. She spoke rarely of herself but much of his mother, mentioning Anselm only in the most casual way.

But "love's young dream" is hopeful after all, and Donald was blessed with a sanguine, trustful nature, so he persuaded himself that the change was perhaps owing to the fact that she was merging into womanhood, and that the time was not far distant when he would return to win her for his very own. That she knew he loved her he did not doubt a moment. She must have guessed his secret from the first and understood his silence. Now that he had passed successfully through his studies and the goal was almost reached, his spirits rose proportionately, and his one impatience was for the day when he would sail for home, for at least she was free to be won. Were it otherwise Anselm would have warned him.

The morning of the commencement dawned brightly, steeping the city in sunshine, yet fanning it with cool breezes that caused the daintily gowned Frenchwomen to don their wraps and the men to walk at a brisker pace than is usual in Paris on a spring morning.

The exercises proved most interesting, and the applause was great as each graduate received his diploma with congratulations from the president of the University.

To Donaldson the whole world seemed full of promise as he and Pierre hastened back to their lodging-house after the closing exercises, glad to throw themselves with lazy contentment into the easy-chairs, arranged with tempting comfort around the room that overlooked somewhat narrow streets, but from which could be seen the bridge and wider thoroughfares.

Donald drew a sigh of satisfaction.

"Well, at last it is over. We are 'doctors' in very truth. Hallo, what is this?" as he spied a white something beside photographs on a table close by. "A letter from home—and mother. I thought it strange I received no word from her to-day."

Involuntarily he looked further about as though searching for another missive; but he looked in vain, and settling himself in the chair again, he scanned the closely written lines. An instant later he rose and went to the window, throwing the blinds wide open, as if to obtain more light, though the

sunshine was streaming in the room, and scru-
tinized each letter of every word as though
unable to believe the evidence of his own
senses. The noise of the streets without,
the presence of Pierre, everything, died out
of his consciousness. Like one stricken
dumb he stood gazing at the letter open in
his hand, then fell heavily forward.

To rush to him, throw wide open his waist-
coat, and dash water into his face, was the
work of an instant for Pierre, but it was many
moments before he could revive him.

"A strain, an overstrain, that is all," murmured Donald faintly; but Pierre, looking into
the pallid face out of which all the light had
gone, could not be deceived, yet felt he dared
not question. A strain. Yes, he thought,
but a strain which will need something more
than time to heal, *mon pauvre ami.*

CHAPTER XXI.

MRS. THORNSDALE's joy at the engagement was unbounded, and she seemed as eager as Anselm himself that it should be brief. Espérance, yielding to their entreaties, consented to be married soon after their return to the city; but Anselm secretly resolved to leave no stone unturned to have the wedding take place before his brother's return in September. Circumstances favored his wish in a most unexpected manner.

Early in August Mrs. Thornsdale was stricken with the same illness which had proved fatal to her husband. Catching a severe cold, pneumonia set in, one of her severe heart spells, to which she had been subject since her husband's death, quickly

137

following. For two days she lingered between life and death, and on the third her
symptoms became so alarming that the physician, as well as Anselm and Espérance,
feared the end might come at any moment.

" If she lives through this day, she will
recover," the doctor told her son; but he gave
but slight hope. The patient herself seemed
convinced that she would never rally, and
calling Espérance to her side, she gently
told her so.

" It is hard to die without seeing my boy,"
she murmured. " Poor Donald! father and
mother both. There is one thing, though,"
she added with a feeble smile, " which would
make me die almost happy," and as Espérance leaned over to catch the words,
the sick woman whispered a request which
caused the girl to start involuntarily.

" Do not refuse," said Anselm's eager voice
beside her; " it is her dying request, my
darling." And Espérance felt indeed that
she could not well hesitate. After all,

whether she were married that day or six weeks later, what mattered it?

"It shall be as you wish, dearest," she said to Mrs. Thornsdale, pressing her lips tenderly to the white face on the pillow. "Anselm will send word at once to Father Searlington." What would he, her old friend, think of the summons, she wondered.

"Have I done well to accede to their wish?" she asked the priest in a hurried whisper, as she joined him for a brief space in an adjoining room an hour later. "She may recover, you know; and the doctor says that this fulfilment of her ardent wish may aid her greatly in the battle of life and death."

"I see no reason why you should not do as she so much desires—poor lady! Do you think you will regret this sudden marriage? You must not be coerced in any way, not even to satisfy the wish of a dying woman," replied Father Searlington, with that keen glance which seemed to penetrate the secret recesses of a soul.

"Oh, no," answered the girl; "it is un-expected, that is all." And then, unbidden by the confessor who had known her since childhood, she knelt on the prie-dieu beside which she was standing, and when Anselm pushed the door softly open a few minutes later, the uplifted hand of the priest and the bowed head he loved so passionately told him that she was receiving the absolution in which she so firmly believed.

"I am ready, quite ready, dear," she said, as, rising, she placed her hand with confidence in his, a great peace shining in her face, and before it the man's soul, with its Judas-stain, trembled guiltily. Espérance wondered why he paled and looked so troubled as he led her to the bedside of his mother, where the physician with Dinah stood ready to act as witnesses.

"For better, for worse; till death do us part." The words, spoken in a low, clear voice, had added solemnity in the sick-room, and as she raised her beautiful, honest eyes to his, Anselm knew that the woman thus giving him her wedded troth was less conscious of those visibly surrounding them than of the invisible Witness in whose name she gave that promise unto death.

*   *   *

And so it was that at eventide a wedding had taken place at Lalla Rookh, and the feeble spark of human life for whose sake it was thus hastened, fanned as it were by the breath of joy, rallying, threw off the .fatal exhaustion. And the little birds sang sweetly their evening song as Espérance Thornsdale looked into her husband's face with a deep content, knowing she had made him happy at last.

Was he altogether happy, or did the trouble of an uneasy conscience mar with unexpected, disturbing force the joy and triumph of his wedding-day?

CHAPTER XXII.

THE days which followed were full of quiet happiness for Espérance. Her husband seemed unable to bear her out of his sight, and her love for him daily increased.

Mrs. Thornsdale convalesced slowly but surely, and was soon counting the days for Donald to be home. Dinah was radiant at having "dear Miss Honey" for a sort of second "Missus," yet, if we could have seen deep down into that faithful heart, we would have read a half regret lingering there that it was not "Massa Donald" who had won the fair girl for his wife. Fond as she was of "Massa Anselm," "Massa Donald" had always been her favorite.

"I always thought Massa Donald cared a heap for Miss Honey, and if he cared once

he cares still, I reckon," she soliloquized.
"He ain't got a heart of mush ready to
squash at the first sight of a pretty face and
then forget all about it," and she shook her
head and looked very bothered.

As the time approached for Donaldson's
arrival, Anselm grew more and more restless. Somehow from the day Espérance
became in reality his, conscience seemed to
awaken and prick him with a certain sense
of shame and uneasiness. It was as if the
intensity of his longing to make her his
wife had blinded him, dulling his realization
of aught else. Since the day he destroyed
his brother's letter and conscience seemed
to die utterly, his one idea had been to win
her affection, to make her irrevocably his
own. Now that he had succeeded and the
fear of losing her was over, and he had
learned the tenderness and depth of her delicate nature, which before he had but half
guessed, he felt abashed, ill at ease as her
trust in him and love for him increased.

Often he would make some pretence and suddenly leave her presence, reluctant though he was to do so even for a moment, as if his guilty soul were oppressed by her spotlessness. His darkness shrank from her light, though it was that very light which deepened and purified the love he bore her, awakening in spite of himself his better nature, causing it to sting with shame beneath the dawning realization of his own despicableness.

Espérance often wondered why he was at times so restless, so excitable, but attributed it to his anxiety about Donald's duplicity and the fear of its effect upon his mother should she learn of his secret marriage. What had become of Donaldson's wife? she herself would often wonder. Did he mean to tell Mrs. Thornsdale upon his return? Would he speak of it, if only in confidence, to Anselm? Occasionally, she would venture some remark to that effect to her husband, but he would grow so disturbed, make so evasive a reply, that she felt instinctively he

was for some reason or other unwilling to
have her allude to the subject in any way,
and as his wish was law to her now in her
deepening love for him, she ceased to speak
of it, wishing much, however, that he would
tell her what was troubling him.

10

CHAPTER XXIII.

IT was drizzling drearily the Sunday Donald was to arrive, as if the heavens were longing to weep freely but could not. The wind sighed in sympathy, chilling the air and deepening the outer gloom. The traveller, however, was not expected until quite late, and as the darkness of evening grew denser, "Lalla Rookh" never looked cheerier, or more homelike. The light of the lamps, the crackling of the wood fires, the very chirp of the crickets breathed welcome.

About seven o'clock Espérance was kneeling before the great fire-place in the library, making the big logs blaze more merrily as they threw fantastic shadows upon the crimson gown of crêpe de Chine which suited her dark beauty so perfectly, and to which the

146

massive mahogany of the antique chairs and
book-shelves formed a fitting background.
Her usually pale face was flushed, and her
eyes shone with the nervous excitement she
could not repress. This home-coming was
strangely different for each one dear to
Donald (Donald himself included, Espérance
thought with mingled pity and scorn) than
either one had anticipated when the young
student left the home circle five years earlier.

How different, she was thinking at that
moment, wondering what new developments
would spring upon them, what the consequences of Donald's unfortunate marriage
would prove to be for his mother as well as
for himself now that he would be home once
more.

"For surely he will tell her now," she
mused, so engrossed in thought that she did
not heed the sound of approaching wheels
till her mother-in-law's voice, as she hastened
down the stairs, startled her.

"There he is now, a whole hour earlier

than we expected!" and a moment later the
mother was clasped in the strong, loving em-
brace of the son and murmuring words almost
incoherent with joy, little dreaming how
much that son needed at that moment the
support of her maternal love and pride.

"My precious, precious boy! What happiness to have you with us again! And
what a great, bearded fellow you are! and
just think, a sister as well as a mother to
welcome you now," with a happy laugh and
all in one breath, unconscious of the sting
her words conveyed as Espérance, hurrying
forward, placed, with an impulse she did not
try to resist, both hands in the outstretched
ones of the man who loved her with such
depth of love.   Did she guess it as she raised
her eyes to his just as she had six years
before when he had welcomed her? No;
but in that brief glance she knew, in spite
of the old smile that lighted his face,
that a great change had passed over Donald Thornsdale, and she pitied him.

"We are glad to have you home once more, Donald, and you have reached us earlier than we expected. Anselm was going to the train to meet you. Ah, here he is this minute," she exclaimed, as his shadow passed the window just then, and in a second more the brothers were face to face.

Anselm blanched deathly white—he could say nothing.

"Well, Anselm, old man, brace up and don't look at me as if I were a ghost," and Donald threw his arm about his brother just as he used when they were boys together, looking at him in a half-amused, yet quizzical way. The words roused Anselm at once.

"Emotion, my dear boy, emotion; you should feel complimented. Maybe it was the beard that staggered me. It quite transforms you. You look quite like a dude—quite à la Parisienne." And going to the other extreme, he talked and joked so incessantly all during supper, which Dinah soon announced (fairly beside herself with joy at having

Massa Don home again), that Espérance watched him anxiously. One would think it was he who had the skeleton in his closet, she thought, without, however, suspecting in the least the truth. But she felt puzzled, and was glad when she was alone with her husband in their own room, hoping, nevertheless, that no ugly skeletons would be unearthed by Donald as he sat conversing till midnight with his mother and thus mar the joy of his return—a joy already tempered by the softened memory of the beloved husband whose proud delight in their boy would have been so boundless.

"Do you know, Anselm, I cannot somehow believe to-night in that clandestine marriage; yet he has suffered in some way; he is not happy in spite of apparent bright spirits— poor Donald!" and she sighed heavily. But her husband made no answer.

Three days later they left "Lalla Rookh" for the city.

CHAPTER XXIV.

THE MYSTERY SOLVED.

ABOUT ten days after Donald's return Anselm was whistling to an accompaniment he was drumming on the piano as Espérance and Donald were conversing desultorily before the large open fire in the library. Mrs. Thornsdale had fallen asleep, knitting in hand. Espérance was always conscious of a slight constraint whenever with Donald. A change had passed over him which perplexed her. There was an uneasiness about him unlike his former self, and at times a look of suffering would cross his face which went to her heart. True, nervousness and mental pain might be the natural outcome of an unquiet conscience, yet somehow she disbelieved more and more the duplicity of which formerly she had deemed him guilty.   Often he would allude to Pierre L'Estrange.   If she could but persuade him to speak unreservedly of his life abroad, at least to her, how much better it would be for all, she thought.

That night his restlessness was more than ever marked, and to Espérance the longing to understand everything was irresistible. Leading the conversation to Paris, she said:

"Tell me more about your life there, will you not?   You speak chiefly, almost entirely, of your studies and work, but little of amusements.   Surely it was not all work and no play?" with a winning smile that covered her anxiety.

"That was just about what it came to," was the quick response.   "My work was altogether my life.   Of course I went to the theatre and opera from time to time both in France and Germany.   L'Estrange and I had many a *tête-à-tête* spree."

"Had not this L'Estrange any family?"

And Donald wondered at the intense, earnest look that accompanied the question.

"Why, yes," he replied, surprised. "Did not Anselm tell you the odd mistake which occurred about his sister's m——"

The drumming stopped with a bang.

"Come, Espérance, get ready," Anselm said with tactless haste. "We will be late for the theatre."

"The theatre!" she exclaimed, astonished. "You did not say anything about going to the play at dinner. It is too late now. See, it is after eight, already."

"True," answered Anselm, looking foolish as the clock struck the half-hour, and Donaldson watched his changing color curiously, a sudden, sharp suspicion darting through his mind. He had noted that Anselm was ill at ease with him ever since the day of his arrival home, and was at a loss to explain it. "Unless it comes from the consciousness that he stole from me the heart of the woman I loved," he thought with bitterness. "Ah, well, that is unjust, I suppose," he would add half aloud. "He did not realize the reality and strength of my affection, and doubtless saw that she was learning to care for him. He must have known at all events that she never loved me, that he was free to win her at least so far as her own heart was concerned, and yet I, poor fool, had dared to hope and think the contrary. Well, all is fair in love and war," and with a poor attempt at a laugh at his own folly, which would end in an impatient sigh, he would dismiss with quick compunction all possible suspicion, however slight, against the honor of the brother of whom he had been both proud and fond. Now, however, he could not silence this keen suspicion. Espérance's earnest question, too, coupled with remarks made at other times, fired his imagination.

"It is altogether too late for the play now," he said quickly. "I was just telling Espérance about the announcements which startled——"

"Espérance, dear, will you run up-stairs and get me the rest of my worsted?" asked Mrs. Thornsdale as naturally as though she had not just been guilty of napping in her chair, a weakness she was always unwilling to acknowledge, much less yield to. There was nothing for the girl to do but to obey, but she wished much that her mother-in-law had not wakened just then.

"Never mind, dearie," cried Mrs. Thornsdale, ascending the stairs a moment later; "I shall have to find it myself. I want to consult you, at all events, about some household matters. Dear me! how sleepy I am to-night," she said, entering her own room where Espérance was searching nervously for the worsted. "I think I won't go down again this evening."

Twenty minutes later Espérance ran downstairs, but the sound of angry voices in the library arrested her. In her alarm she involuntarily paused.

The instant his mother had left the room

Donald confronted Anselm standing irresolutely beside the piano.

"Why did you not tell Espérance of the odd mistake about that marriage. There was some reason for your silence. What was it?"

"Reason! Absurd. It was not worth speaking of—a mere silly blunder!" with a forced laugh, but changing color very perceptibly beneath his brother's penetrating gaze. "Pshaw! I am lazy, too, to-night," with a pretended yawn. "I guess I shall follow Espérance's example and——"

"No, you shall not; at least, not yet," said Donald coolly, laying a firm hand upon his arm. "There is some mystery. Mystery has been in the very air I breathed ever since my return home. The evening of my arrival, when I reached here earlier than you expected, you turned deathly white, with a look of consternation that has haunted me ever since—equalled only by your terror now—you are trembling like a leaf."

"Confound you! Let go of my arm.

You love her yourself even now when she is no longer free, and the consciousness of it makes you suspicious." But Donald heeded not the taunt and held him as in a vise.

"I find her watching me at times with a curious, distrustful expression," he mused aloud, yet more to himself than to the other. "Whenever the subject of Paris is broached, the name of L'Estrange mentioned, that strange look invariably comes. Tell me, did Espérance see those announcements when they first were published in the *Herald?*"

"No, she did not," and Donald knew he had given him the lie.

"I shall ask her. I shall not have long to wait," and he dropped the arm he had held so tightly.

Anselm was checkmated. If he begged him not to ask that question, it would but reveal the fact that there was something to conceal. If it were asked, his honor would be shattered, and forever, before the wife just learning to love him so deeply.

"You shall not ask her.   What will you gain by making her suffer?" too excited to realize that his own words confirmed the other's worst forebodings.

"You admit then there is something to cause her suffering?"   The words sounded hard and measured.   "I see it all.   You, my brother, knew I loved her, and through jealousy you made her believe I was false to her."   Then raising his voice just as Espérance's light footstep touched the stairs, he cried out: "Do you think I will stand quietly by and let her, the woman I have loved with all the strength of my being, believe that lie—believe that I have deceived her, been false to her?   Not while there is breath in my body to speak will I keep silent."

"Speak, then," answered Anselm passionately, "expose me if you will.   She is mine, mine at all events.   Nothing can alter that fact.   Espérance, cost her what it may, will never be unfaithful to her marriage vow, never."

"And you depended upon that.   Coward!
If you were not my brother, I'd——"   But
the sentence was never finished, for Espérance, after a second of unconscious hesitation,
threw back the portières and stood confronting them upon the threshold.

"Anselm! Donald! what does this mean?"
she cried, her voice clear as a bell.   "What
mean those words I have just heard?"

But neither answered.   Dumbfounded, the
brothers stood speechless before her, Anselm
with bowed head and shamed face, Donald
erect though anxious, with a strange eagerness in his face.

"Quick, Anselm, what is it?" she again
repeated, hastening to her husband's side.
"What do you mean by exposure?   Why
do you speak of my faithfulness to my marriage vow—and to Donald?"   Her voice faltered a little then, but Anselm bent his head
lower still.   He dared not face her, and his
shame spoke more eloquently than words of
guilt.   She looked helplessly up at Donald,

so proud yet so eager, and in his face read the love of all these years—love and a great pity, and in its light the truth dawned upon her.

"I have done you an injustice, Donald—forgive me." The words were almost a whisper, but the pain in the sweet voice, the pathetic drooping of the head, went straight to his heart, making him forgetful of himself, of everything save her happiness. In a flash he realized the truth of Anselm's words.

"Do not be alarmed, Espérance," he answered hurriedly then. "Anselm and I have had a misunderstanding, and in the heat of argument we were carried away by excitement. It is over, quite over, is it not, Anselm?" But Espérance's earnest gaze never left his face.

"I cannot be deceived now, Donald," she said gently. "Leave me with my h—with Anselm."

And Donald, leaving the room, left husband and wife together.

CHAPTER XXV.

AN EARLY VISIT TO THE RECTORY.

SLEEPLESS, Espérance rose almost at dawn, and as early as seven o'clock reached the rectory in Sixteenth Street, just as the Angelus bell rang out clear and distinct in the frosty air.

Father Searlington, alarmed at the early summons, hastened to the room where Espérance awaited him with feverish eagerness. Hurriedly and as briefly as possible, she told him her trouble and perplexity.

"Is there no redress, Father? no possible escape for me? I know I can never be free in the full sense of the word, but am I, in duty bound, compelled to live as his wife, as——" but her voice faltered.

"My poor child," murmured the priest; then after a second of silence, he said firmly:

"Those whom God hath joined together no human power can put asunder."

"But there are cases where the Church permits separation," she interrupted.

"True; but only in extreme cases, rare exceptions, one of which Christ Himself alludes to in the Gospel of St. Matthew—limiting separation even in that case by clear pronunciation of the fearful sin of which either husband or wife would be guilty were either to marry again during the other's lifetime; condemnations repeated in the tenth and sixteenth chapters of the Gospels of Mark and Luke. Under the old law, marriage, though solemn, was a contract which could permissibly, even if not advisably, by mutual consent, be broken like other contracts. Since the God-man came upon earth and raised matrimony to the dignity of a sacrament, likening it to His own indissoluble union with His 'spouse,' the Church, that Church cannot, except in cases of extremest urgency, sanction anything which would interfere, however slightly, with the natural and supernatural consequences of the sacred bond of marriage now rendered divine."

Father Scarlington then spoke of individual circumstances where legal separation would be a *necessity* in order to insure protection from the state, the Catholic husband or wife clearly understanding that neither was free in the sight of God to marry.

"Your case is indeed a sad one; you and his brother have been basely deceived by your husband. But he is still your husband, and your duty, hard though it is, is clear. No assistance from the state is necessary; no physical, temporal harm can reach you, and, my daughter, no moral evil either. Pain, mental anguish, yes, but no moral evil."

"And Donald, Donald," she murmured, with an accent of inexpressible sadness. "What will become of him? If it were but a question of my own personal suffering, I could more easily forgive. Father Searlington, you spoke of no moral evil coming to

me. Are you sure? I am weak, and I shall
be tempted, so tempted. Ah, what shall I
do?"

> "At the cross her station keeping,
> Stood the mournful Mother weeping
> Close to Jesus till the last."

The words sung by the sweet voices of the
children that Lenten morning reached her
distinctly.

"She, the Mother human, though sinless,
stood beneath the cross. Child, there is your
answer. You must not merely kneel, but
stand beneath this heavy cross, close to Him
who has never failed you, who will never fail
you. Courage! You are a Christian, with
interests to guard far higher than that of
mere personal happiness—the honor of Him
who is your supreme Lord and King, the
spiritual life of human souls He died to redeem. The treachery which has cruelly
brought grief and disappointment to your
heart has grieved, more deeply even than you,
One who has loved this soul, now so sick

with moral weakness, since eternity. Nurse that sick soul for His sake, my child. Let your faithfulness to duty, cost what it may, bring not only peace to yourself, as it surely will sooner or later, but light and healing to the very one who has wronged you and to the brother whom he has stricken. Any sacrifice, however great, is after all but little to make for love of your Saviour, and the day will come—it cannot be very long even at the uttermost—when the sharpest pain will have its contented and everlasting rest."

Espérance was silent. She could not speak, but the light on her face told the priest that his appeal was not in vain. And kneeling for a few moments in the chapel close by, she hastened, strengthened if not yet consoled, back to the home now suddenly become her Calvary.

CHAPTER XXVI.

DUTY'S CALL.

"Good morning, chérie," said Mrs. Thornsdale as Espérance entered the dining-room a little later. "Anselm raced down-town before breakfast, and Don, after a hurried cup of coffee, hastened away also, leaving only me to welcome you this bright morning," and she kissed her daughter, as she always called her son's wife, with tender affection, as the girl stooped for the usual caress. "You must have been to a very early Mass; you look tired, dear."

"Yes, I did not sleep very well last night," Espérance answered quickly, but so quietly and naturally that Mrs. Thornsdale suspected nothing.

How she stood the ordeal of the usual small-talk at the breakfast table, mechani-

cally forcing herself to eat whatever was placed
before her, she herself wondered. There
was the customary discussion about minute
plans for the day, comments upon the morning news, and the girl's heart shrank when
Mrs. Thornsdale asked her to go shopping
with her that forenoon. Just then a shrill
voice was heard at the front door, evidently
arguing some question with Dinah.

"Yes, she does live here too, I tell you,"
a high childish voice was saying. "2 Madison Square, that's the number she gave me;
but I'll be flumbergasted if I can remember her
name. Oh, I've got it, it's Clerk—the Clerk."

"The Clerk!" gasped Dinah. "Well, I
reckon you are flumbergasted, whatever that
state may be, young man. Can't you say Le
Clerque? It ain't difficult; just try," said
Dinah, now thoroughly amused, but Espérance, recognizing the voice as that of her
little protégé at the hospital, Tim O'Reilly,
hastened forward.

"Why, Tim, is that you? I am glad to

see you; so you are really out at last.
Come in and tell me all about yourself. Are
you able to walk comfortably?" And then
followed a lengthy conversation in which her
mother-in-law, with great amusement and her
usual kindliness, joined, Tim soon leaving,
with his pockets fuller than they had ever
been before with "goodies," as he expressed
it, his childish heart fairly bursting with
pride and delight, and making Espérance's
own heart lighter for the kindness with which
she had cheered the little unfortunate. But
the shopping tour soon commenced, small
household duties had to be attended to, and
as the day dragged wearily on, a numb, bewildered sense of wrong and sorrow rested
upon her as she mechanically fulfilled the
routine of petty duties, only the almost
deathly whiteness of her face betraying any
external sign of uncommon agitation. Dinah's keen eyes indeed detected something
unusual about "Mrs. Honey," as she affectionately styled her in her quaint dialect,

something "queer-like" about "Massa Anselm," and her faithful heart was troubled.

"'Massa Donald' didn' even say 'good
morning, Dinah,'" she soliloquized. "He
didn' read the newspapers, nor drink his coffee, nor nothin', and 'Massa Anselm'—well,
he looked sick as he could look, and 'Mrs.
Honey' looks as white as a ghost and kinder
blank at times. Somethin's wrong, Dinah,
somethin's wrong." But she wisely kept her
own counsel and bided her time.

Five o'clock brought a telegram from Anselm, saying he was detained and would not
be home till late that evening. Espérance
was scarcely surprised, though the tact which
prompted him to send the message as usual
to her instead of to his mother, as he had been
wont to do before their marriage, did surprise
and relieve her, too. All through that sad
day she realized more and more strongly, and
with a pang of self-reproach for not remem-
bering it clearly from the first, the impera-
tiveness of guarding Mrs. Thornsdale against

the slightest suspicion of the estrangement between the sons she so loved. Grieved and shocked indeed would be that warm, generous heart were she to learn of the treachery, the mean deceit, and selfishness of her youngest-born, her pride, her darling, with the consequences so full of pain to Donald and Espérance. " I must do my duty if only for her sake," thought the young wife; " she must be spared grief at any cost." And the resolution gave added gentleness to her loving ways with the kindly woman who had proved in truth a mother to the friendless girl.

And Donald, how had he spent the day? she wondered. Would he too not return till night? Something told her he would be faithful to his post whatever came. Nor was she mistaken. At the usual time, he returned for office duty, from four to six in the afternoon; yet it was not professional duty alone which brought Donaldson home. Throughout the wakeful night and during the hospital work of the morning, a resolve was strengthening. The light in Espérance's face the evening before when she learned his integrity, the depth of his love which hesitated at no sacrifice, haunted him. In it he read that not only was her heart his in the past, but that now, Anselm's wife though she was, it would be his again and for-ever, had he but the right to claim it. And had he not that right? Surely before God and man she was his; no longer Anselm's since he had basely deceived her. Not even the Catholic Church, so strict in regard to everything pertaining to the marriage bond, could consider her bound to one who had proved himself so unworthy of her trust.

Thus he reasoned, a feeling of triumph mingling with the sharp pain of his brother's treachery, the indignation and horror with which it filled him. Just as the office hours were ending, he received an urgent call to a patient out of town. For an instant he stood irresolute. Then, writing a few hasty lines to Espérance, he rang for Dinah, bidding her carry the note at once. " I am called out of town to an urgent case which will detain me forty-eight hours. I will not go unless I first see you, Espérance. The train leaves shortly. It must rest with you."

Espérance read the words hurriedly, frightened at their vehemence, but she did not hesitate a moment.

" Say I will be down at once, Dinah," and in a few minutes she entered Donald's office, pale but strangely composed; yet the man started at the change which grief had worked already in the young face that to him was always the most beautiful one in the world. The sight of her suffering made him desperate.

" You sent for me, Donald," she said softly, though her voice trembled a little. " You surely cannot hesitate. It is duty's call."

" Duty's call, yes. But I have another duty to perform also, Espérance, the duty of protecting you, you who have been, and ever will be, the love of my life, from the man whose treachery has brought such misery——"

She interrupted him with a low cry of deprecation that was almost terror; but he heeded it not, almost unconsciously barring the door by standing directly in front of it.

"Listen, Espérance," he said, trying to speak more calmly, but with a determination which it was plain nothing would cause to swerve. "You must listen this once at least. You owe it to me, if only in memory of the love which, seeking your best and truest interest, made me silent when I longed to speak during the years I waited and worked and—prayed for you; prayed, do you hear me, Espérance, that you might be mine at last, that I might so live as to be not altogether unworthy of you."

"Oh, hush, hush, you must not speak to me like this. I am not free to listen to such words as these. Oh, have pity!"

The last words broke from her involuntarily

as she felt the fearfulness of the strain in witnessing his tenderness and pain.

Her sorrow and purity abashed him.

"I will never ask you to go against your conscience. I love and reverence you far too much to ask or wish you to do so. But, Espérance, my little Espérance"—ah, how the words vibrated through her inmost soul! —"have you no duty towards me, no pity for me? Is it possible that you are still in conscience bound to remain the wife of one who has cruelly deceived not only me, but you; who won your affection under false pretences, only to pain you at last; who——"

"I married Anselm for better, for worse. I will be faithful to him, as I promised, until death. Your goodness to me, your consideration of me in the past, I can never repay— ah, do not think that I do not appreciate it; but, oh, show your respect for me now by helping me to do my duty."

The cry was almost a whisper. Her limbs trembled so that she sank instinctively into the chair beside her, unable to stand a moment longer.

"As for you, Donald," she continued, after a brief pause, "I pity you from the depth of my heart. But you, as well as I, must be loyal."

"Loyal to the man who outraged me, who robbed me of the woman I lo——"

"Loyal to conscience, Donald," she interrupted firmly; "loyal to the higher law in which we both believe. Anselm has been base indeed, but I am his wife; a wife's wedded promise should be and ever will be respected by a noble man like you, for you are noble, brave-hearted, true—good in every sense of the word. You will be faithful to your high calling and learn to live down both the anguish and the—the love—for one who has no right to receive it."

She rose resolutely as she spoke, but he put his hand out to detain her.

"And there is no hope for me, Espérance—none?" he asked in a dull, helpless way.

"None," she answered.   "It is useless to speak further."   But his despair went to her heart; she could not bear to leave him in such utter misery.

"Courage, Donaldson; remember you have a glorious mission in life.   Even now while you tarry, a suffering fellow-creature is waiting your coming.   Your mission is to heal, soothe, sustain, even though your own heart is crushed and bleeding, even—remember— as the divine Physician sustained and comforted others when bowed beneath the burden of personal woe."

Her voice grew clearer and stronger as she spoke, and a light that was more than human shone on her face.   Before it the man's soul was awed.   He tried to speak further but could not, and, passing him quickly, she reached her room, and threw herself on her knees before the ebony crucifix in that mute suffering so much deeper than any other; words she had lately read coming to her as she knelt struggling there:

"Beneath the shelter of Thy cross,
I kneel, O Lord Divine.

. . . . .

And though 'tis hard to bear the load,

. . . . .

And battle 'gainst the foe

. . . . .

Still, when I look upon Thy face

. . . . .

And gaze upon Thy wasting form,

. . . . .

Oh! then the sorrows of my life
Fade beneath those of Thine."

12

CHAPTER XXVII.

MECHANICALLY Donald boarded the train which was to carry him to the town from which the summons had come; mechanically, yet correctly, he prescribed for the patient, and then, regardless of the pelting rain and piercing wind, went straight from the house of sickness out into the driving storm—a storm far worse than that of mere material elements was raging within his soul, setting mind and heart and brain on fire. The roads were strange, but he staggered on; how far he did not know or care. Suddenly he supported himself with quick instinct of self-preservation against some stone steps, as a tremendous gust of wind struck him with such force as to take him, strong man as he

178

was, nearly off his feet. As the hurricane
subsided he looked up and, confronting him
like a silent monitor, were the gray walls of
a church, some distance from the village.
Almost unconsciously Donald mounted the
steps, and pushing open the heavy door, entered the edifice, enshrouded in utter darkness save for the dim light of the sanctuary
lamp and the gleam of the white altar. For
an instant he stood like one bewildered, then,
groping forward in a dazed kind of way, he
fell on his knees with a cry that seemed to
echo and re-echo.

"Out of the depths have I cried unto Thee,
O Lord! Lord, hear my cry!"

Hardly had the words rung forth when,
hearing a slight noise, he looked up, startled.
Had some other storm-tossed soul entered
that sacred haven for refuge from self and
sin and sorrow? No. It was only a priest
coming to bring the Viaticum to some dying
person, unconscious that any one was there.
Donald could see by the light of the taper

which the priest placed on the altar that he
genuflected before the Tabernacle, which he
opened, taking out the golden chalice, and
placing something—what, Donald did not then
comprehend—in a small dark case; then he
shut the little gilded door, and descended the
altar steps.   As he did so the rays of the
taper he carried fell full upon his upturned
face, and Donald saw reflected there such
worship, such calm, that the memory of it
lingered with him in after life like a bene-
diction.

"My God! what faith, what love," he murmured, and the silent example of belief divine helped to bring peace to his fevered
spirit.   Gradually the gentler, more softened
feeling of grief overcame him, and bowing
his head, the strong man sobbed like a child
at the feet of Him whose own tears have
sanctified human weeping forever.

*   *   *

That same night Espérance, hearing again
the ceaseless pacing in the adjoining room,

rose with determination, and pushed open the door.

"Anselm, you must come and rest; you are tired," and as he turned quickly at the sound of her voice, she fell at his feet, for the first time in all those hours of anguish losing consciousness.

CHAPTER XXVIII.

HUSBAND AND WIFE.

EARLY the next morning Anselm pushed softly open the door leading to his wife's room. Was she asleep? he wondered. The closed lids, the even, gentle breathing, and perfect motionlessness answered him. For some minutes he stood mutely watching her, a strained look on his set countenance. The very pose of the head, as it rested upon the pillow, the listlessness of the outstretched arms, the utter stillness of the slender form, suggested complete exhaustion. There was a weariness in the young face even as she slept that went to his heart, lines which spoke of suffering that aged it.

"It will kill her," he murmured; "she will not complain, but it will kill her, and I shall be her murderer."

Yet he made no actual outcry, but threw his arms upward in an unconscious gesture, as if to supplicate some Unseen Power, yet not daring to pray. There could be no mercy for such as he, either above or on earth. She stirred and her eyes opened with a frightened, questioning look.

"Is that you, Anselm? Do you want anything?"

"You must not go down to breakfast." The prosaic words sounded forced and unnatural. "Dinah will bring your coffee upstairs."

"Oh, no; I will not be a moment. Is it late?"

"You must rest; I insist upon it. Promise me you will not make the effort. I will tell mother you are not well." And seeing his feverish anxiety, she promised, and he turned to leave the room. Suddenly he returned.

"Espérance," he said, speaking quickly, "I did not mean to trouble you this morning.

I intended waiting till later when you would be stronger, but it is useless. I cannot live through this day, too, in silence. You are my wife. I know your stern sense of duty, but I want to say that, if it is in my power to make you free, I will do so."

His voice choked, but he went on, heedless of her deprecating cry. "I have deliberately deceived you; married you under false pretences. I do not wish your life to be marred forever because of my wickedness. True, I should have thought of that before, but I considered nothing, weighed nothing, save the appalling probability of losing you irrevocably, and I could not, would not bear it, for I loved you with an intensity impossible to conceive."

He paused, only the chirping of a little bird that had lighted on the window-sill breaking the stillness of the room.

"After our marriage, when I knew that you were mine, my very own, that all possibility of losing you was over, I seemed gradu-

ally to realize my perfidy. Your uplifting
life, your confidence in my uprightness, put
me to shame. I began to fear discovery,
the effects of my deception upon you, and
the fear poisoned the sweetness, the blessed-
ness of our new life together."

The last words were almost inaudible.

"I will do what I can to free you; it is
the only reparation I can make to you—
both."

"And do you think I could ignore my
wedded promise?" she asked gravely. "Your
sin against your brother is greater even than
against me, greater still against your Maker;
but I am yours, Anselm. Nothing in this
life can sever us. Never shall I, in thought,
word, or deed, be disloyal to my vow. I am,
and ever shall be your wife in every sense
of the word, your friend and helpmate, come
what will, till death do us part, my husband."

The words sounded as clear as the day she
first gave him her troth, and the Searcher of

all hearts alone knew the depth of struggle and pain out of which that promise was given the second time, the sunlight streaming through the casement resting upon her like the smile of God.

CHAPTER XXIX.

FORTITUDE.

THE young wife was faithful indeed to her promise. Had she protested in angry words against his treachery, spoken in scathing language to him, been gloomy or selfish beneath her wrong and grief, or were she by nature incapable of much spirit, Anselm would have felt less poignantly his own baseness and would have been more or less on the defensive. Her dignity from the first utterly disarmed him. Her brave, uncomplaining silence, her quiet endeavor to lessen as far as possible the constraint between the brothers, to be as bright and merry as ever with their mother—now hers also—to act simply and naturally in every way as before, although suffering acutely herself, made his remorse more keen and unbearable, rendered

worse by the consciousness that he had
wrecked the happiness of an innocent man—
his brother and companion since childhood.
He saw, too, Donald's unselfish consideration
of Espérance in every way, and gauged at
last the immense depth and purity of his
affection for her, and it put his own love to
shame. Espérance gauged it too, and it
taunted her the more as she felt that Anselm's affection was not what she would have
wished, since it failed to prevent him stooping to so low a moral level. Her pure nature, deepened by the exquisite spirituality
of a true and perfect faith, shielded her, in
one sense, from temptation to which a nature less high, less upheld by religion, might
have been subjected under such trying circumstances; but she was conscious that the
love which she had once given Donaldson,
now that she knew him to be all that she
once believed him, was threatening to spring
to life again with overpowering vitality; that
love for another, however elevating in itself

it might be, would be sin, since she was
no longer free. Nothing could alter the
fact that she was Anselm's wife, wedded to
him for better, for worse; that no man could
put asunder those whom God hath joined.
Though he had forfeited her respect and affection by his own baseness, she was nevertheless forbidden to give her heart's loyalty
to another, however noble; bound by solemn
vow to be faithful through life to him with
whom she was one in a union which death
alone could sever.

As for Donaldson, he did not even pre-
tend to forgive. How could he pardon
such treachery on the part of the brother
whom he had loved and trusted since boy-
hood? Yet for the sake of Espérance and
his mother, he exchanged common civilities
with him when in their presence, even conversing with him, in a general way, when
circumstances necessitated it. He did what
he could, with a delicacy born of love, to
spare Espérance as much as possible. Often

he would slip away in the evening on plea of
study or professional duty, and the girl would
try to still the involuntary regret at his absence, the quickening of her heart at his approach.

She resolutely avoided Donald whenever
feasible, and when compelled to be with him,
avoided discussions which might even inad-
vertently suggest thoughts relative to the
strained relations between themselves and her
husband. Her tact in turning the drift of
conversation when it was trenching on dan-
gerous ground showed the keen sensitiveness
of the woman's instinct, that made her quick
also in detecting the slightest faithlessness,
however involuntary, to her wedded promise,
even within the secrecy of her most hidden
thoughts. To consciously dwell upon what
might have been—that were she free, she
would be Donald's, not Anselm's wife, would
be in itself a disloyal act, for what is thought
but the action of the mind? A realm, visible
indeed to none save One, but which can easily

shelter sin, dimming in a second the sunlight of purity, truth, and charity within the
soul, even if no outward act follow.   But the
struggle which was going on in the very quick
of her nature told pitiably upon her physical
strength.   The sweet face grew paler and
thinner, and the slender form so fragile that
both Anselm and Donald became seriously
anxious.   Mrs. Thornsdale noted it also, but
attributing it to some passing cause, felt con-
fident that the country air was all she needed.
And thus the weeks glided on, and Espérance
came to a decision which never swerved.
She must go away with her husband, not only
for her own sake and his, but for Donald's.
It was sweet, too dangerously sweet, to be
near him whose deeply tried love for her she
knew so well and whose noble nature was so
congenial to her own—too trying a test to
him to have her there.   She felt rightly that
this was a case where safety was in flight.

"He who loveth the danger shall perish in it."

The words of Scripture with warning voice
often recurred to her. It would not do to
trifle with temptation as a moth does with a
candle. Donald could not be the one to go.
His professional duties, his mother, rendered
it impossible; so broaching the subject gradually to her husband, she begged him to take
her abroad, back once more to the home of
her childhood.

CHAPTER XXX.

It was a glorious morning, six weeks later, when Espérance Thornsdale boarded "*La Bretagne*," the gay steamer which was to carry her miles away from at least immediate temptation, if not from sorrow.

They knew no one on board except in a casual way—a relief to Anselm as well as to his wife, who after the first day was on deck most of the quiet voyage. Anselm unobtrusively did all he could to make her comfortable in every way, still avoiding, as he did at home, any attempt to inflict his companionship upon her. Ever present, with its sense of bitter humiliation and pain, was the conviction that, however gentle and loyal she might strive to be, his presence could not but be painful and a strain upon her.

13   193

And he guessed rightly. Without losing a moment the stern self-repression which was slowly undermining her health, there were moments when the realization—the keener in her isolation on the steamer—of the baseness of which she and Donald were victims filled her with shuddering horror, that threatened to overpower her; moments when indignation and rebellion at having been thus meanly tricked into marrying Anselm made it well nigh impossible to control an involuntary shrinking from him—a shrinking intensified by the thought that the love he bore her could not have been in its nature all that she had believed it to be, since it failed in making him superior to such despicableness. Yet she was sorry for him too. She was too true a woman not to feel pity for pain, however deserved; too impregnated with the teachings of her Master, Christ, to permit any feeling of vengeance which her nature, strong though so gentle, was capable of experiencing, prevail to harden her to the agony which was writing more deeply every day those haggard lines in his youthful countenance.

She forced herself to look forward, upward, not backward, unless to cling to what she knew had been white in that life before the blackness of crime had cast its hideous mask upon it, and tried to picture to herself what that character might yet become through the purifying influence of a sincere repentance.

"Nurse that sick soul for His sake." The words of the priest rang like a refrain of pleading tenderness that was more than human in her heart, keeping it free from bitterness, filling it with mercy; and the calm expanse of the mighty sea about her breathed promise of an endless peace.

One night, unable to sleep, she rose from her berth and, throwing a long cloak over a warm wrapper of some white texture, she went outside to get the air. It was rougher than usual and the deck seemed deserted. Where was Anselm, she wondered. It was his custom to come to her state-room from time to time to inquire if she needed anything, but that evening he had not been near her and she began to feel vaguely troubled.

Looking anxiously up and down, her glance fell upon a dark figure standing with folded arms in the most forsaken corner of the deck. Drawing nearer, she distinguished by the light of the moon the features of her husband, but features whitened in a look of such awful despair as he stood gazing like one fascinated at the dark waters gleaming in the moonlight beneath, that a sudden suspicion seizing her, the cry " Anselm, my husband!" broke unbidden from her, startling him from his lethargy.

"Well," he said doggedly, the strange, dulled expression still on his face, yet reading the unspoken question of the troubled eyes raised in terror to his, " what would it matter? Your life is wrecked and his. It is far better for me to end it all and set you free, free, do you understand?" he said with sudden vehemence, "to marry the brother I robbed. I would have paid my debt, made my restitution and found——"

"What?" asked the quiet, awe-stricken voice by his side. And, looking from the surging waters beneath to the woman he loved, then back again to that vast ocean of seething waves, he repeated mechanically, "What, indeed?"

Could the surging sea give peace to his fevered spirit? Was there a power in heaven itself which could still that maddening remorse, that suffocating humiliation of soul before the bar of his own conscience that was such torture even when alone?

And Espérance divined his thoughts even as he had hers. With gentleness inexpressible she spoke of hope, of the possibility of redemption even on this earth, of life and love—the God-love that, unwilling to mock a contrite soul with a half-hearted forgiveness that would leave still upon it the ugly stain of its sin, instituted a sacrament divine through which the foulest stains can be wiped away even in this life—the love that means in truth "crowned, not vanquished when it says forgiven."

"You do not believe that now, but you will some day, and in the meanwhile trust my pity, dear."

And Anselm, in a dazed sort of way, let her lead him as unresisting as a child to the room below. She supported him rather than he her as they descended the stairs amid the heaving of the boat, and, making him lie down, she bathed his burning forehead with refreshing water and knelt beside him, his hot hand in her cool one, till he fell into an exhausted sleep; as she saw him resting at last, she raised her pure face upward with an expression of mingled thankfulness and pleading.

"O Thou who aidest me, a weak creature, to forgive, deign Thou to forgive also; shelter within Thy limitless pity this soul Thou didst die to redeem."

CHAPTER XXXI.

ABROAD.

LITTLE did the gay people who met the husband and wife during their travels suspect the hidden tragedy in those two lives so closely linked together. To strangers they appeared merely an attractive-looking couple, apparently devoted to one another, though the husband was considered by common verdict so morose a man that it was surprising so beautiful and brilliant a girl as his young bride could have fallen in love with him, more than one secretly wondering why she seemed restless if separated from him for any length of time.

Espérance was, in fact, nervous if Anselm left her for more than a short while. That terrible experience on the steamer revealed the morbid condition of his mind, and made

her realize that not only did he suffer, but
that he suffered far more than either herself
or Donaldson, for they were spared the gnaw-
ing pain of a fruitless remorse of conscience,
however deeply they sorrowed.

Anselm guessed her fear, and it touched
him to the quick.   How pathetically faithful,
how brave she was!   Yet he dared not take
her in his arms as he longed, and tell her how
he worshipped her—he was not fit.   But, one
day, when he noticed the unconscious look of
relief as he entered her room after leaving
her for an entire morning, he did tell her
with stern self-condemnation that she need
not worry; that there was no fear of his being
a coward a second time.   "For cowardice it
was," he exclaimed passionately.   "Life
seemed unbearable, chiefly because I had to
face each moment the consequences of my
own wickedness."

And she answered him with soothing
words, as was her wont, and did her duty
simply, day by day, praying that peace

might come at last to this tortured soul, as well as to the loyal heart that had loved her so nobly across the sea.

Donald's secret, in the meanwhile, had been guessed, at least in part, by the one nearest to him in the world. The mental strain had been great upon him, and the day Espérance sailed for Europe, as he strove to reply to his mother's exclamation of how desolate the house seemed without her bright presence, something in the tone of his voice made her look quickly at him, and, seeing the pain in his face, she hurried to his side and put her arms around him, just as she did when he was only a child--the mother-heart had divined her boy's sorrow at last, though the treachery of the other was sealed to her forever.

CHAPTER XXXII.

" NON SUM DIGNUS."

THE countless waterfalls fell with refreshing murmur over the rocky edges, tempting Espérance to drink of the pure water, as she and Anselm drove through the pass leading into Italy.

The Simplon! What memories of interest throng each step of the way!

More than once Espérance insisted upon alighting and, stooping, curved the palm of her hand to drink of the crystal falls, making a lovely picture in the gray gown which fitted her so perfectly, a jaunty toque of a deeper shade set daintily on her shapely head. The scenery about them made a fitting setting for her striking beauty. Her moral strength was like the rugged mountains towering above her, mused her husband; her ten-

derness and unconscious grace like the exquisite delicacy of the vales, blushing with
the wild bloom of their varied shrub and
flower, in soft contrast to the austere gran-
deur of the snow-capped peaks.

Through Maggiore, Lugano, Como, they
travelled, conversing little, as they drank in
every detail of the wondrous beauty of sky
and hill and lake; thence onward to Rome.

The sunlight was tipping the Colosseum
with gold, as if to compensate with its bright-
ness the gloomy memories of its historic
walls, as the travellers entered the city of
ages.

How Espérance's heart thrilled as she
crossed the threshold of the Eternal City!
How little did it seem to matter whether joy
or sorrow was her portion in this fleeting
life. There, within reach of the great heart
of spiritual truth—vivifying in spite of the
discord of an unjust persecution—was the visible heart from which flowed a love, light and
power, that clothed human souls with a moral

beauty never seen on earth before, its uplifting touch destined to purify unto the end of
time the most defiled, if only they will enter
within its fold divine.

Through the influence of one of the leading cardinals to whom they had letters of
introduction they soon received invitations to
a Papal audience. It was dark and cloudy
when they started in the early morning, but
just as they reached the Vatican the clouds,
breaking, revealed a silver lining, sure pres-
age of the sunlight which later would flood
the city with radiance. Would the clouds
overhanging their lives thus disperse, wondered Espérance. To her, engrossed not so
much with the present as with the past life
of that wonderful Power which, witnessing
the changing and passing away of all human
things, remains itself unchanging and in-
destructible, the waiting in the audience-
chamber seemed but a short while, but to
Anselm it was interminable. He watched,
indeed, with keen interest every detail of

the ceremonial surrounding them, but its very impressiveness suffocated him. Nothing escaped him—the respectful attitude and earnest attention of each visitor, Catholic or otherwise; the black court dresses and veils of the women contrasting vividly with the scarlet flowing garbs of the cardinals; the white-robed commanding figure of the Pontiff standing out in bold relief, as he murmured words in foreign language, now to one stranger, then to another, kneeling to give, at least, outward respect to the office a pure-hearted old man was filling with such humble dignity.

More restless every moment grew Anselm as the significance of each imposing detail forced itself upon his quickened perceptions. How could guilty youth dare so much as to kneel at the feet of holy age? A Judas-stained soul dare receive a blessing from the Vicar of uncreated holiness?

Did the penetrating gaze of the Father of all Christians, as it lingered an instant upon that troubled countenance, read something of

the struggle within? Anselm never learned;
but beneath that gaze, piercing yet so kind,
the shadow of a mercy that is infinite seemed
to enfold his sin-wearied spirit within its own
tender pity.

"*Non sum dignus,*" the words were almost
a whisper, and the wife only knew that as he
stooped to receive the grace of that blessing
he bent his head very low; and as she, too,
knelt in loving homage beside him, she raised
her pure face to the aged one above her:

"*Daignez—priez pour lui.*"

CHAPTER XXXIII.

AFTER SEVEN YEARS.

THE sunlight was glancing on the water, the " swish," " swish" of the waves murmuring merrily at one of the seaside resorts not far from New York, one morning, seven years after our heroine's memorable visit abroad. Were we to have caught a momentary glimpse of her as she sat that bright day close to the sea, clad in a simple gown, a wide-brimmed hat protecting her from the sun, we should have thought that in spite of the vicissitudes of that long interval she was much the same Espérance of earlier years. It was not a sad face which watched with loving pride the winsome play of a little girl about four years of age, building sand-houses beside her; but there was a depth in the dark eyes that gave to it beauty inexpressible; an indescribable something that only suffering brings, the after-glow of grief nobly borne.

Young as she still was, one felt that her heart had sounded depths of human pain and struggle, drawing from thence peace—not bitterness; light—not darkness.

" *Viens vite, chérie;* the water will wet you."

" The waves are playing tag with me; *vois, Maman!*" cried the child, clapping her tiny hands with glee.

" See who is coming, *ma petite.* Run and meet dear grandma." But little Pauline needed no bidding: spying the form of a white-haired lady scanning the beach in search of them, she flew as fast as her small feet could carry her, her pink sun-bonnet hanging down her back, revealing golden-brown curls and two big dimples that invited one to kiss the piquant face at once. Mrs. Thornsdale evidently thought so, for she fairly smothered the little one with kisses.

"A letter from Uncle Don, my pet," she cried so Espérance could hear, and holding the letter up so she could see it.

"Containing special news, I suppose?" queried her daughter-in-law as she rose to greet her, with a half mischievous, inquiring glance.

"News, hardly," she replied in a musing way. "He speaks of his patient doing well, the cruise as delightful."

"And nothing of Miss Faith?" interrupted Espérance, a shade of disappointment crossing her face.

"Oh, yes; he speaks of Faith. I scarcely know what to think. My child, read the letter," she said with sudden earnestness. "I want you to see what he says," and Anselm's wife, slowly perusing its pages, read the following:

Dearest Mother:
The cruise is most delightful in every way, my patient reviving under the strong sea-air remarkably. His sister is one of the

most charming elderly women I have ever
met, and Miss Faith is like a ray of veritable
sunshine to each one. Her devotion to her
invalid father is touching. No; there is
nothing between us except a very true friendship. I have no right to offer the dregs of a
heart to any woman, much less to one like
her. You understand what I mean, mother
mine. The affection lived down only because it had no right to longer exist; the
suffering which time alone helped to heal,
has left scars which can never be wholly ef-
faced. I am simply incapable of affection in
that form—a settled-down bachelor in very
truth, and Miss Faith's own heart was buried
years ago in a soldier's grave in some distant
land—she is twenty-seven now, you know.
I sometimes wonder whether the future might
not develop possibilities which neither of us
anticipate, but at present we are only good
comrades, each sympathizing with the other
without any actual explanation from either.
You see I am quite frank, for I know your
wish. Well, after all, I am not much to be
pitied. I have my profession, which I seem
to love more and more each day. Come what

will, I have you, dearest mother, and the soul-satisfying truth—how satisfying, morally, intellectually one can learn only from experience—which *she*, our star of hope, was the first to lead me to seek. I can never think of her as anything but a bright ray that has helped me in spite of darkness, and, indeed, every one who has come beneath her influence. Faith reminds me of her.

In Paris I saw my old friend, Pierre L'Estrange and his boys. Tell Espérance that I have seen a jointed doll which I mean to send Pauline, but that it is to be a surprise from "Uncle Don," whom the little fairy condescends to love in spite of seeing him so rarely. Write me by return mail the latest decision of the oculist respecting Anselm's eyes. Give him my love and tell him he must remain in the air all day.

"Well, what do you think of it, my dear?" asked Mrs. Thornsdale, as Espérance, slowly folding the letter, handed it to her.

"Think? Why, that our 'settled-down bachelor' is fast becoming a benedict," was the quick reply, with an arch smile that

covered how deeply the letter had touched
her.

"Ah, Monsieur Frère," she said to herself
in an odd little way, "methinks you are finding in more senses than one that there is
something besides *espérance* in this life—
la foi." But she became silent, almost pen-
sive.

She thought of how she had given Donald
the first freshness of her girlish affection,
how grieved she had been when he had
seemed to be weak and fickle, how slowly
she had learned to care for his brother, and
then as wife-love came and deepened within
her, how she had awakened to the realization
of the baseness of the one to whom she had
pledged her troth till death. The interior
struggle of mind and soul rose before her
with that sudden retrospection which comes
unbidden at certain moments in each human
life. But as she dwelt upon the inward peace
which her fidelity to duty brought to her own
heart, of the light and healing which it had

carried to the two hearts which had loved her
—differently, yet so ardently—of her little
child who was the sunshine of her life, she
was more than content. Amid the darkness
of loss and treachery she had led him who
had loved her nobly to the One who alone
can soothe even the stormiest tempest of human pain. The spotlessness of her life had
been the searchlight by which a sin-dyed
soul had seen reflected its own despicableness, becoming through the cleansing waters
of a veritable contrition and reparation as
"white as snow," one with her in faith and
fortitude at last.

"If only his sight were restored, it is all
I could wish—my poor Anselm! Ah, there
he is," she exclaimed aloud, "and alone,"
and she hurried anxiously to meet him.

"Alone! Is that safe, Anselm?" she exclaimed, looking with eager anxiety at the
handsome face, which, unlike her own, had
aged greatly in those past seven years. The
hair was gray above the temples, though he

was not much over thirty, but there was an air of nobility about him that formerly he had lacked.

" Quite safe, dearest. I want to show you how independent I can be," he said with a little laugh that was not free from sadness. " One of the men led me to the beach and then I was all right."

" We have news from Donald," she said later, as they stood alone by the water's edge. " I think he and Faith Shandon will come together before very long. He sends his love to you and says you must stay out in the air all day."

Simple words, but they sent the blood rushing to his face, lighted with a flash of sudden joy.

" Forgiven, in very truth," he murmured.

" Forgiven long ago, my husband; only you could not realize it even after you had sacrificed—these," and she touched caressingly the eyes unable to see the glory of the deepening twilight on the sea.

"That was simple justice," was the quiet reply. "Even the night of the fire when I felt that blinding heat as I climbed to save him, I realized that the sacrifice of sight itself was a poor compensation for the wrong I did him in robbing him of you. My loss is less great than his. O my wife! it may be that I will one day see again; but if not, I will have you to help me bear my expiation bravely to the end. Come what may, I will have you with me till death do us part."

"And after," murmured the wife, and with tenderness unspeakable she looked into the blind face above her, the light in it telling of the chastened spirit, rendering him in humble trustfulness like "unto a child," fit for the kingdom of Heaven—and Espérance.

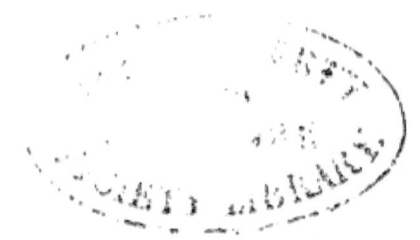

PRINTED BY BENZIGER BROTHERS, NEW YORK.

Standard Catholic Books

BENZIGER BROTHERS,

CINCINNATI:	NEW YORK:	CHICAGO:
343 MAIN ST.	36 & 38 BARCLAY ST.	178 MONROE ST.

ABANDONMENT; or, Absolute Surrender. 32mo, *net*, o 40

ALTAR BOY'S MANUAL, THE LITTLE. Illus. Small 32mo, o 25

ANALYSIS OF THE GOSPELS. Lambert. 12mo, *net*, 1 25

ART OF PROFITING BY OUR FAULTS. 32mo, *net*, o 40

BIBLE, THE HOLY. 12mo, cloth, 1 25

BIRTHDAY SOUVENIR, OR DIARY. 32mo, o 50

BLESSED ONES OF 1888. 16mo, illustrated, o 50

BLIND FRIEND OF THE POOR : Reminiscences of the Life and Works of Mgr. de Segur. 16mo, o 50

BLISSYLVANIA POST-OFFICE, THE. By M. A. Taggart. 16mo, o 50

BONE RULES; or, Skeleton of English Grammar. By Rev. J. B. Tabb. 16mo, *net*, o 35

BOYS' AND GIRLS' MISSION BOOK. By the Redemptorist Fathers. 48mo, o 35

BOYS' AND GIRLS' ANNUAL. o 05

BROWNSON, ORESTES A., Literary, Scientific, and Political Views of. By H. F. Brownson. 12mo, *net*, 1 25

BUGG, LELIA HARDIN. The Correct Thing for Catholics. 16mo, o 75

—— A Lady. Manners and Social Usages. 16mo, 1 00

BY BRANSCOME RIVER. By M. A. Taggart. 16mo, o 50

CANTATA CATHOLICA. Containing a large collection of Masses, etc. Hellebusch. Oblong 4to, *net*, 2 00

CATECHISM OF FAMILIAR THINGS. 12mo, 1 00

CATHOLIC BELIEF; or, A Short and Simple Exposition of Catholic Doctrine. By the Very Rev. Joseph Faà di Bruno, D.D. 200th Thousand. 16mo.
Paper, 0.25; 25 copies, 4.25; 50 copies, 7.50; 100 copies, 12.50
Cloth, 0.50; 25 copies, 8.50; 50 copies, 15.00; 100 copies, 25.00

"When a book supplies, as does this one, a demand that necessitates the printing of one hundred thousand [now two hundred thousand] copies, its merits need no eulogizing." —*Ave Maria.*

CATHOLIC CEREMONIES and Explanation of the Ecclesiastical Year. By the Abbé Durand. With 96 illustrations. 24mo.
Paper, 0.25; 25 copies, 4.25; 50 copies, 7.50; 100 copies, 12 50
Cloth, 0.50; 25 copies, 8.50; 50 copies, 15.00; 100 copies, 25 00

A practical, handy volume for the people at a low price. It has been highly recommended by Cardinals, Archbishops, and Bishops.

CATHOLIC FAMILY LIBRARY. Composed of "The Christian
Father," "The Christian Mother," "Sure Way to a
Happy Marriage," "Instructions on the Commandments
and Sacraments," and "Stories for First Communicants."
5 volumes in box.   2 04

CATHOLIC HOME ANNUAL.   0 25

CATHOLIC HOME LIBRARY. 10 volumes. 12mo, each, 0 45
    Per set,   3 00

CATHOLIC WORSHIP. The Sacraments, Ceremonies, and
    Festivals of the Church Explained. 32mo, Paper, 0.15;
    per 100, 9.00. Cloth, 0.25; per 100,   15 00

CATHOLIC YOUNG MAN OF THE PRESENT DAY. Egger. 32mo,
    0.25; per 100,   15 00

CHARITY THE ORIGIN OF EVERY BLESSING. 16mo,   0 75

CHILD OF MARY. A complete Prayer-Book for Children of
    Mary. 32mo,   0 60

CHRIST IN TYPE AND PROPHECY. Maas. 2 vols. 12mo, *net*, 4 00

CHRISTIAN ANTHROPOLOGY. Thein. 8vo,   *net*, 2 50

CHRISTIAN FATHER, THE. Paper, 0.25; per 100, 12.50. Cloth,
    0.35; per 100,   21 00
    " 'The Christian Father' is a very useful work. It should
be in the hands of every Christian Father, as 'The Christian
Mother' should be carefully read by every mother who loves
her children."—F. S. Chatard, Bishop of Vincennes.

CHRISTIAN MOTHER, THE. Paper, 0.25; per 100, 12.50. Cloth,
    0.35; per 100,   21 00
    " I had to stop reading from time to time to utter a strong
prayer to our good God, that every mother could have a copy
of the book, 'The Christian Mother.' "—J. J. Lynch, Archbishop of Toronto.

CIRCUS-RIDER'S DAUGHTER, THE. A novel. By F. v. Brackel.
    12mo,   1 25

CLARKE, REV. RICHARD F., S.J. The Devout Year. Short
    Meditations. 24mo,   *net*, 0 60

COBBETT, W. History of the Protestant Reformation. With
    Notes and Preface. By Very Rev. F. A. Gasquet, D.D.,
    O.S.B. 12mo,   *net*, 0 50

COCHEM'S EXPLANATION OF THE MASS. With Preface by Rt.
    Rev. C. P. Maes, D.D. 12mo, cloth,   1 25
    This work is compiled from the teachings of the Church, of
the early Fathers, of theologians, and spiritual writers. It is
written in an agreeable and impressive manner, and cannot
fail to give the reader a better acquaintance with the Mass,
and to inflame him with devotion for it.

COMEDY OF ENGLISH PROTESTANTISM, THE. Edited by A. F.
    Marshall. 12mo,   *net*, 0 50

COMPENDIUM SACRAE LITURGIAE, Juxta Ritum Romanum.
    Wapelhorst. 8vo,   *net*, 2 50

CONFESSIONAL, THE. By Right Rev. A. Roegel, D.D. 12mo,
                                                 net, 1 00

2

CONNOR D'ARCY'S STRUGGLES. A novel. By Mrs. W. M. Bertholds. 12mo, 1 25

COUNSELS OF A CATHOLIC MOTHER to Her Daughter. 16mo, 0 50

CROWN OF MARY. A complete Manual of Devotion for Clients of Mary. 32mo, 0 60

CROWN OF THORNS, THE; or, The Little Breviary of the Holy Face. 32mo, 0 50

DATA OF MODERN ETHICS EXAMINED, THE. Ming. 12mo, *net*, 2 00

DAY OF FIRST COMMUNION. Paper, 5 cents; per 100, 3 00

DE GOESBRIAND, RIGHT REV. L. Christ on the Altar. 4to, richly illustrated, gilt edges, 6 00
—— Jesus the Good Shepherd. 16mo, *net*, 0 75
—— The Labors of the Apostles. 12mo, *net*, 1 00

DEVOTIONS AND PRAYERS BY ST. ALPHONSUS. A complete Prayer-Book. 16mo, 1 00

EGAN, MAURICE F. The Vocation of Edward Conway. A novel. 12mo, 1 25
—— The Flower of the Flock, and The Badgers of Belmont. 12mo, 1 00
—— How They Worked Their Way. 12mo, 1 00
—— A Gentleman. 16mo, 0 75
—— The Boys in the Block. 24mo, leatherette, 0 25

ENGLISH READER. Edited by Rev. Edward Connolly, S. J. 12mo, 1 25

EPISTLES AND GOSPELS. 32mo, 0 25

EUCHARISTIC CHRIST, THE. Reflections and Considerations on the Blessed Sacrament. By Rev. A. Tesnière. Translated by A. R. Bennett-Gladstone. 12mo, *net*, 1 00

EUCHARISTIC GEMS. A Thought about the Most Blessed Sacrament for Every Day in the Year. Coelenbier. 16mo, 0 75

EXAMINATION OF CONSCIENCE for the use of Priests. Gaduel-Grimm. 32mo, *net*, 0 30

EXPLANATION OF THE BALTIMORE CATECHISM. Kinkead. 12mo, *net*, 1 00

EXPLANATION OF THE GOSPELS of the Sundays and Holydays. With an Explanation of Catholic Worship. 24mo, illustrated.
Paper, 0.25; 25 copies, 4.25; 50 copies, 7.50; 100 copies, 12 50
Cloth, 0.50; 25 copies, 8.50; 50 copies, 15.00; 100 copies, 25 00
"It is with pleasure I recommend the 'Explanation of the Gospels and of Catholic Worship' to the clergy and the laity. It should have a very extensive sale; lucid explanation, clear style, solid matter, beautiful illustrations. Everybody will learn from this little book."—ARCHBISHOP JANSSENS.

EXPLANATION OF THE COMMANDMENTS, ILLUSTRATED. By Rev. H. Rolfus, D.D. With a Practice and a Reflection on each Commandment. By Very Rev. F. Girardey, C.SS.R. 16mo, 0 75
This is a very interesting and instructive explanation of the Commandments of God and of the Church, with numerous examples, anecdotes, etc.

3

EXPLANATION OF THE OUR FATHER AND THE HAIL MARY
Adapted by Rev. Richard Brennan, LL.D. 16mo,   0 75

EXPLANATION OF THE PRAYERS AND CEREMONIES OF THE
MASS, ILLUSTRATED. By Rev. I. D. Lanslots, O.S.B.
With 22 full-page illustrations. 12mo,   1 25
Clearly explains the meaning of the altar, of its ornaments,
of the vestments, of the prayers, and of the ceremonies per-
formed by the celebrant and his ministers.

EXPLANATION OF THE SALVE REGINA. By St. Alphonsus
Liguori. 16mo,   0 75

EXTREME UNCTION. Paper, 10 cents; per 100,   5 00
The same in German at the same prices.

FABIOLA; or, The Church of the Catacombs. By Cardinal
Wiseman. Illustrated Edition. 12mo,   1 25
Edition de luxe,   6 00

FATAL DIAMONDS, THE. By E. C. Donnelly. 24mo, leatherette,   0 25

FINN, REV. FRANCIS, J., S.J. Percy Wynn; or, Making a Boy
of Him. 12mo,   0 85

——— Tom Playfair: or, Making a Start. 12mo,   0 85

——— Harry Dee; or, Working it Out. 12mo,   0 85

——— Claude Lightfoot; or How the Problem was Solved.
12mo,   0 85

——— Ethelred Preston; or, The Adventures of a Newcomer.
12mo,   0 85

——— That Football Game; and What Came of It. 12mo, 0 85

——— Mostly Boys. 12mo,   0 85

——— My Strange Friend. 24mo, leatherette.   0 25
Father Finn's books, are, in the opinion of the best critics,
standard works in modern English literature; they are full
of fascinating interest, replete with stirring and amusing incidents of college life, and admirably adapted to the wants of
our boys.

FIRST COMMUNICANT'S MANUAL. Small 32mo,   0 50

FIVE O'CLOCK STORIES. 16mo,   0 75

FLOWERS OF THE PASSION. 32mo   0 50

FOLLOWING OF CHRIST, THE. By Thomas à Kempis. With
Reflections. Small 32mo, cloth,   0 50
Without Reflections. Small 32mo, cloth,   0 45
Edition de luxe. Illustrated,   from 1 50 up.

FRANCIS DE SALES, ST. Guide for Confession and Communion. 32mo,   0 60

——— Maxims and Counsels for Every Day. 32mo,   0 50

——— New Year Greetings. 32mo, flexible cloth, 15 cents;
per 100,   10 00

GENERAL PRINCIPLES OF THE RELIGIOUS LIFE. Verheyen.
32mo,   net, 0 30

GLORIES OF DIVINE GRACE. Scheeben. 12mo,   net, 1 50

GLORIES OF MARY, THE. By St. Alphonsus Liguori. 2 vols.
12mo   net, 2 50

GOD KNOWABLE AND KNOWN. Ronayne. 12mo,   net, 1 25

4

GOFFINE'S DEVOUT INSTRUCTIONS. Illustrated Edition. With Preface by His Eminence Cardinal Gibbons. 8vo, cloth, 1.00; 10 copies, 7.50; 25 copies, 17.50; 50 copies, 33 50

This is the best, the cheapest, and the most popular illustrated edition of Goffine's Instructions. As a work of spiritual reading and instruction this book stands in the foremost rank. In it the faithful will find explained in a plain, simple manner the doctrines of the Church, her sacraments and ceremonies, as set forth in the Epistles and Gospels.

"GOLDEN SANDS." Books by the Author of. Golden Sands. Little Counsels for the Sanctification and Happiness of Daily Life. 32mo.

Third Series,   o 60
Fourth Series,   o 60
Fifth Series,   o 60

Also in finer bindings.

—— Book of the Professed. 32mo.

Vol. I. }
Vol. II. } Each with a Steel-Plate Frontispiece. { *net*, o 75
Vol. III. }   { *net*, o 60
   { *net*, o 60

—— Prayer. Offered to Novices and Pious People of the World. 32mo,   *net*, o 40

—— The Little Book of Superiors. 32mo,   *net*, o 60
—— Spiritual Direction. 32mo,   *net*, o 60
—— Little Month of May. 32mo, flexible cloth,   o 25
—— Little Month of the Souls in Purgatory. 32mo, flexible cloth,   o 25
—— Hints on Letter-Writing. 16mo,   o 60

GROU, REV. N., S.J. The Characteristics of True Devotion. Edited by Rev. Samuel H. Frisbee, S.J. 16mo,   *net*, o 75

—— The Interior of Jesus and Mary. Edited by Rev. Samuel H. Frisbee, S.J. 16mo, 2 vols.,   *net*, 2 00

HAMON'S MEDITATIONS. See under Meditations. 5 vols. 16mo,   *net*, 5 00

HANDBOOK FOR ALTAR SOCIETIES, and Guide for Sacristans. 16mo,   *net*, o 75

HANDBOOK OF THE CHRISTIAN RELIGION. By Rev. W. Wilmers, S.J. From the German. Edited by Rev. James Conway, S.J. 12mo,   *net*, 1 50

HAPPY YEAR, A; or, The Year Sanctified by Meditating on the Maxims and Sayings of the Saints. Lasausse. 12mo,   *net*, 1 00

HEART, THE, OF ST. JANE FRANCES DE CHANTAL. Thoughts and Prayers. 32mo,   *net*, o 40

HEIR OF DREAMS, AN. By S. M. O'Malley. 24mo, leather-ette,   o 25

HELP FOR THE POOR SOULS IN PURGATORY. Small 32mo, o 50

HIDDEN TREASURE; or, The Value and Excellence of the Holy Mass. By St. Leonard of Port-Maurice. 32mo,   o 50

HISTORY OF THE CATHOLIC CHURCH. By Dr. H. Brueck. 2 vols., 8vo,   *net*, 3 00

HISTORY OF THE CATHOLIC CHURCH. Brennan-Shea. Illus. 8vo,   1 50

HISTORY OF THE MASS and its Ceremonies. O'Brien. 12mo, *net*, 1 25

HOLY FACE OF JESUS, THE. Meditations on the Litany of the Holy Face. 32mo, 0 50

HOURS BEFORE THE ALTAR. De La Bouillerie. 32mo, 0 50

HOW TO GET ON. Feeney. 12mo, 1 00

HOW TO MAKE THE MISSION. By a Dominican Father. 16mo, paper, 10 cents, per 100, 5 00

HUNOLT'S SERMONS. *Complete Unabridged Edition.* Translated by the Rev. J. Allen, D.D. 12 vols., 8vo, *net*, 30 00

Vols. 1, 2. The Christian State of Life.
Vols. 3, 4. The Bad Christian.
Vols. 5, 6. The Penitent Christian.
Vols. 7, 8. The Good Christian.
Vols. 9, 10. The Christian's Last End.
Vols. 11, 12. The Christian's Model.

His Eminence Cardinal Gibbons, Archbishop of Baltimore: ". . . Should find a place in the library of every priest. . . ."

His Eminence Cardinal Vaughan, Archbishop of Westminster: ". . . I cannot praise it too highly. . . ."

HUNOLT'S SHORT SERMONS. *Abridged Edition.* The Sermons arranged for all the Sundays. 5 vols., 8vo, *net*, 10 00

IDOLS; or, The Secret of the Rue Chaussée d'Antin. A novel. By Raoul de Navery. 12mo, 1 25

ILLUSTRATED PRAYER-BOOK FOR CHILDREN. 32mo, 0 35

IMITATION OF THE BLESSED VIRGIN MARY. After the Model of the Imitation of Christ. Translated by Mrs. A. R. Bennett-Gladstone. 32mo, 0 50
Edition de luxe. Illustrated. from 1.50 up.

INSTRUCTIONS ON THE COMMANDMENTS and the Sacraments. By St. Liguori. 32mo, paper, 0.25; per 100, 12.50; cloth, 0.35; per 100, 21 00

This excellent and pious little manual, written by one of the greatest doctors of the Church, is an almost indispensable acquisition to every Catholic that desires worthily to receive the sacraments and to observe faithfully the Ten Commandments of God.

KONINGS, THEOLOGIA MORALIS. Novissimi Ecclesiæ Doctoris S. Alphonsi. In Compendium Redacta, et Usui Venerabilis Cleri Americani Accommodata, Auctore A. Konings, C.SS.R. Editio septima. 2 vols. in one, half mor., *net*, 4 00

—— Commentarium in Facultates Apostolicas. New, enlarged editon. 12mo, *net*, 2 25

—— General Confession Made Easy. 32mo, flexible, 0 15
The same in German at the same price.

LAMP OF THE SANCTUARY. A tale. By Cardinal Wiseman.
48mo, leatherette,   0 25

LEGENDS AND STORIES OF THE HOLY CHILD JESUS from
Many Lands. A. Fowler Lutz. 16mo,   0 75

LEPER QUEEN, THE. A Story of the Thirteenth Century.
16mo,   0 50

LETTERS OF ST. ALPHONSUS LIGUORI. Centenary Edition.
5 vols., 12mo, each,   *net*, 1 25

LIBRARY OF THE RELIGIOUS LIFE. Composed of "Book of
the Professed," by the author of "Golden Sands," 3 vols.;
"Spiritual Direction," by the author of "Golden Sands;"
and "Souvenir of the Novitiate." 5 vols., 32mo, in
case,   3 25

LIFE AND ACTS OF LEO XIII. Keller. Illustrated, 8vo,   2 00

LIFE OF ST. ALOYSIUS GONZAGA. Cepari-Goldie. Edition de
luxe. 8vo,   *net*, 2 50

LIFE OF FATHER CHARLES SIRE. 12mo,   *net*, 1 00

LIFE OF ST. CLARE OF MONTEFALCO. 12mo,   *net*, 0 75

LIFE OF THE VEN. MARY CRESCENTIA HÖSS. 12mo, *net*, 1 25

LIFE OF ST. FRANCIS SOLANUS. 16mo,   *net*, 0 50

LIFE OF FATHER FRANCIS POILVACHE. 32mo, paper, *net*, 0 20

LIFE OF ST. GERMAINE COUSIN. 16mo,   0 50

LIFE OF ST. CHANTAL. See under "St. Chantal."   *net*, 4 00

(LIFE OF) MOST REV. JOHN HUGHES. Brann. 12mo, *net*, 0 75

LIFE OF FATHER JOGUES. Martin-Shea. 12mo,   *net*, 0 75

LIFE OF MLLE. LE GRAS. 12mo,   *net*, 1 25

LIFE OF MARY FOR CHILDREN. 24mo, illustrated,   *net*, 0 50

LIFE OF RIGHT REV. JOHN N. NEUMANN, D.D. 12mo, *net*, 1 25

LIFE, POPULAR, OF ST. TERESA. 12mo,   *net*, 0 75

LIFE OF CHRIST. Illustrated. By Father M. v. Cochem.
Adapted by Rev. B. Hammer, O.S.F. With fine half-tone
illustrations. 12mo,   1 25

LIFE OF THE BLESSED VIRGIN. Illustrated. Adapted by Rev.
Richard Brennan, LL.D. With fine half-tone illustrations.
12mo,   1 25

LIFE OF OUR LORD AND SAVIOUR JESUS CHRIST and of His
Blessed Mother. Brennan. Illustrated.

> No. 1. Roan back, gold title, plain gold sides, sprinkled
> edges,   *net*, 5 00
>
> No. 3. Morocco back and corners, cloth sides with gold
> stamp, gilt edges,   *net*, 7 00
>
> No. 4. Full morocco, richly gilt back, with large figure
> of Our Lord in gold on side, gilt edges,   *net*, 9 00
>
> No. 5. Full morocco, block paneled sides, superbly gilt,
> gilt edges,   *net*, 10 00

LINKED LIVES. A novel. By Lady Douglas. 8vo,   1 50

LITTLE CHILD OF MARY. Large 48mo,   0 25

LITTLE MANUAL OF ST. ANTHONY. Illustrated. 32mo,
cloth,   0 60

LIGUORI, ST. ALPHONSUS DE, Complete Ascetical Works of. Centenary Edition. Per volume, *net*, 1 25

Each book is complete in itself, and any volume will be sold separately.

Preparation for Death.
Way of Salvation and of Perfection.
Great Means of Salvation and Perfection.
Incarnation, Birth, and Infancy of Christ.
The Passion and Death of Christ.
The Holy Eucharist.
The Glories of Mary, 2 vols.
Victories of the Martyrs.
True Spouse of Christ, 2 vols.

Dignity and Duties of the Priest.
The Holy Mass
The Divine Office.
Preaching.
Abridged Sermons for all the Sundays.
Miscellany.
Letters, 4 vols.
Letters and General Index.

LITTLE OFFICE OF THE IMMACULATE CONCEPTION. Paper, 3 cents; per 100, 1 50

LITTLE PICTORIAL LIVES OF THE SAINTS. With Reflections for Every Day in the Year. With nearly 400 illustrations. 12mo, 1 00
10 copies, 6.25; 25 copies, 15.00; 50 copies, 27.50; 100 copies, 50 00

This book has received the approbation of the following prelates: Archbishop Kenrick, Archbishop Grace, Archbishop Hennessy, Archbishop Salpointe, Archbishop Ryan, Archbishop Gross, Archbishop Duhamel, Archbishop Kain, Archbishop O'Brien, Archbishop Katzer, Bishop McCloskey, Bishop Grandin, Bishop O'Hara, Bishop Mullen, Bishop Marty, Bishop Ryan, of Buffalo; Bishop Fink, Bishop Seidenbush, Bishop Moreau, Bishop Racine, Bishop Spalding, Bishop Vertin, Bishop Junger, Bishop Naughten, Bishop Richter, Bishop Rademacher, Bishop Cosgrove, Bishop Curtis, and Bishop Glorieux.

LITTLE PRAYER-BOOK OF THE SACRED HEART. Sm. 32mo, cloth, 0 40
Also in finer bindings.

LITTLE SAINT OF NINE YEARS. De Ségur. 16mo, 0 50

LOURDES. Clarke. 16mo, Illustrated, 0 75

LUTHER'S OWN STATEMENTS. O'Connor. 12mo, paper, 0 15

MANIFESTATION OF CONSCIENCE. Confessions and Communions in Religious Communities. 32mo, *net*, 0 50

McCALLEN, REV. JAMES A., S S. Sanctuary Boy's Illustrated Manual. 12mo, *net*, 0 50

—— Office of Tenebræ. 12mo, *net*, 1 00

—— Appendix. Containing Harmonizations of the Lamentations. 12mo, *net*, 0 75

MANUAL OF INDULGENCED PRAYERS. A complete Prayer-Book. Small 32mo, cloth, 0 40
Also in finer bindings.

MANUAL OF THE HOLY EUCHARIST. Conferences and Pious
Practices, with Devotions for Mass, etc. Undertaken at
the particular instance of the Very Rev. Director-General of
the Priests' Eucharistic League, and prepared by Rev. F. X.
Lasance. Director of the Tabernacle Society of Cincinnati.
Oblong 24mo.   o 75

Also in finer bindings.

MANUAL OF THE HOLY FAMILY. 32mo, cloth,   o 60
Also in finer bindings.

MARCELLA GRACE. A novel. By Rosa Mulholland. Illustrated. 12mo,   1 25

MARRIAGE. Monsabré, O.P. 12mo,   *net,* 1 00

MAY DEVOTIONS, NEW. Reflections on the Invocations of the
Litany of Loretto. 12mo,   *net,* 1 00

MEANS OF GRACE, THE. A Complete Exposition of the Seven
Sacraments, of the Sacramentals, and of Prayer, with a
Comprehensive Explanation of the "Lord's Prayer" and
the "Hail Mary." By Rev. Richard Brennan, LL.D.
With 180 full-page and other illustrations. 8vo, cloth, 2 50;
gilt edges, 3.00; Library edition, half levant,   3 50
"The best book for family use out."—Bishop Mullen.

MEDITATIONS (HAMON'S) FOR ALL THE DAYS OF THE YEAR.
For the use of Priests, Religious, and the Laity. By Rev.
M. Hamon, S.S. From the French, by Mrs. Anne R.
Bennett-Gladstone. 5 vols., 16mo,   *net,* 5 00
"The five handsome volumes will form a very useful
addition to the devotional library of every ecclesiastic."—His
Eminence Cardinal Logue.

"Hamon's doctrine is the unadulterated word of God,
presented with unction, exquisite taste, and freed from that
exaggerated and sickly sentimentalism which disgusts when
it does not mislead."—Most Rev. P. L. Chapelle. D.D.

MEDITATIONS (CHAIGNON, S.J.) FOR THE USE OF THE SECU-
LAR CLERGY. By Father Chaignon, S.J. From the French,
by Rt. Rev. L. de Goesbriand, D.D. 2 vols., 8vo, *net,* 4 00

MEDITATIONS (BAXTER) for Every Day in the Year. By Rev
Roger Baxter, S.J. Small 12mo,   *net,* 1 25

MEDITATIONS (PERINALDO) on the Sufferings of Jesus Christ.
Perinaldo. 12mo,   *net,* o 75

MEDITATIONS (VERCRUYSSE) for Every Day in the Year.
Vercruysse. 2 vols.,   *net,* 2 75

MEDITATIONS ON THE PASSION OF OUR LORD. 32mo,   o 40

MISSION BOOK OF THE REDEMPTORIST FATHERS. 32mo,
cloth,   o 50

MISSION BOOK FOR THE MARRIED. By Very Rev. F. Girardey,
C.SS.R. 32mo, cloth,   o 50

MISSION BOOK FOR THE SINGLE. By Very Rev. F. Girardey,
C.SS.R. 32mo, cloth,   o 50

MISTRESS OF NOVICES, The, Instructed in her Duties. Leguay.
12mo, cloth,   *net,* o 75

MOMENTS BEFORE THE TABERNACLE. Russell. 24mo, *net,* o 40

MONK'S PARDON. A Historical Romance. By Raoul de
Navery. 12mo, 1 25

MONTH OF THE DEAD; or, Prompt and Easy Deliverance of
the Souls in Purgatory. 32mo, 0 75

MONTH OF MAY. Debussi. 32mo, 0 50

MONTH OF THE SACRED HEART. Huguet. 0 75

MONTH, NEW, OF MARY, St. Francis de Sales. 32mo, 0 40

MONTH, NEW, OF THE SACRED HEART, St. Francis de Sales.
32mo, 0 40

MONTH, NEW, OF ST. JOSEPH, St. Francis de Sales.
32mo, 0 40

MONTH, NEW, OF THE HOLY ANGELS, St. Francis de Sales.
32mo, 0 40

MOOTED QUESTIONS OF HISTORY. By H. Desmond. 16mo, 0 75

MR. BILLY BUTTONS. A novel. By Walter Lecky. 12mo, 1 25

MÜLLER. REV. MICHAEL, C.SS.R. God the Teacher of
Mankind. 9 vols., 8vo. Per set, *net*, 9 50
The Church and Her Enemies. *net*, 1 10
The Apostles' Creed. *net*, 1 10
The First and Greatest Commandment. *net*, 1 40
Explanation of the Commandments, continued. Precepts
of the Church. *net*, 1 10
Dignity, Authority, and Duties of Parents, Ecclesiastical
and Civil Powers. Their Enemies. *net*, 1 40
Grace and the Sacraments. *net*, 1 25
Holy Mass. *net*, 1 25
Eucharist and Penance. *net*, 1 10
Sacramentals—Prayer, etc. *net*, 1 00
• Familiar Explanation of Catholic Doctrine. 12mo, 1 00
—— The Prodigal Son; or, The Sinner's Return to God.
8vo, *net*, 1 00
—— The Devotion of the Holy Rosary and the Five
Scapulars. 8vo, *net*, 0 75
—— The Catholic Priesthood. 2 vols., 8vo, *net*, 3 00

MY FIRST COMMUNION: The Happiest Day of My Life.
16mo, illustrated, 0 75

NAMES THAT LIVE IN CATHOLIC HEARTS. Cardinal
Ximenes—Michael Angelo—Samuel de Champlain—Archbishop Plunkett—Charles Carroll—Henry Larochejacque-
lein—Simon de Montfort. By Anna T. Sadlier 12mo, 1 00

NEW RULE OF THE THIRD ORDER. 32mo, 5 cents;
per 100, 3 00

NEW TESTAMENT, THE. Illustrated edition. With 100 fine
full-page illustrations In two colors. 16mo, *net*, 0 60

The advantages of this edition over others consist in its
beautiful illustrations, its convenient size, its clear, open type,
and substantial and attractive binding. It is the best adapted
for general use on account of its compactness and low price.

OFFICE, COMPLETE, OF HOLY WEEK. Latin and English.
24mo, cloth, 0.50; cloth, limp, gilt edges,   1 00
Also in finer bindings.

O'GRADY, ELEANOR. Aids to Correct and Effective Elocution. 12mo,   1 25

—— Select Recitations for Schools and Academies. 12mo, 1 00
—— Readings and Recitations for Juniors. 16mo, *net*, 0 5>
—— Elocution Class. A Simplification of the Laws and
Principles of Expression. 16mo,   *net*, 0 50

ON CHRISTIAN ART. By Edith Healy. 16mo,   0 50

ON THE ROAD TO ROME, and How Two Brothers Got There.
By William Richards. 16mo,   0 50

ONE AND THIRTY DAYS WITH BLESSED MARGARET MARY.
32mo, flexible cloth,   0 25

ONE ANGEL MORE IN HEAVEN. With Letters of Condolence
by St. Francis de Sales. White mar.,   0 50

OUR BIRTHDAY BOUQUET. Donnelly. 16mo,   1 00

OUR FAVORITE DEVOTIONS. By Very Rev. Dean A. A.
Lings. 24mo,   0 60
While there are many excellent books of devotion, there
is none made on the plans of this one, giving ALL the devotions in general use among the faithful. It will be found a
very serviceable book.

OUR FAVORITE NOVENAS. By Very Rev. Dean A. A. Lings.
24mo,   0 60
Gives forms of prayer for all the novenas to Our Lord,
the Blessed Virgin, and the Saints which pious custom has
established.

OUR LADY OF GOOD COUNSEL IN GENAZZANO. By Anne R.
Bennett, née Gladstone. 32mo,   0 75

OUR OWN WILL, and How to Detect it in Our Actions. Allen.
16mo,   *net*, 0 75

OUR YOUNG FOLKS' LIBRARY. 10 volumes. 12mo, each, 0 45;
per set,   3 00

OUTLAW OF CAMARGUE, THE. A novel. By A. De Lamothe.
12mo,   1 25

OUTLINES OF DOGMATIC THEOLOGY. By Rev. Sylvester J.
Hunter, S.J. 3 vols., 12mo,   *net*, 4 50

PETRONILLA, and other Stories. Donnelly. 12mo,   1 00

PEW-RENT RECEIPT BOOK. 800 receipts.   *net*, 1 00

PHILOSOPHY, ENGLISH MANUALS OF CATHOLIC.

Logic. 12mo,   *net*, 1 25
First Principles of Knowledge. 12mo,   *net*, 1 25
Moral Philosophy (Ethics and Natural Law). 12mo, *net*, 1 25
Natural Theology. 12mo,   *net*, 1 50
Psychology. 12mo,   *net*, 1 50
General Metaphysics. 12mo,   *net*, 1 25
A Manual of Political Economy. 12mo,   *net*, 1 50

PARADISE ON EARTH OPENED TO ALL. 32mo, *net*, 0 40

PASSING SHADOWS. A novel. By Anthony Yorke. 12mo, 1 25

PEARLS FROM FABER. Selected and arranged by Marion J. Brunowe. 32mo, 0 50

PICTORIAL LIVES OF THE SAINTS. With Reflections. 8vo, 2 00
  5 copies, 6.65; 10 copies, 12.50; 25 copies, 27.50; 50 copies, 50 00

POPULAR INSTRUCTIONS ON MARRIAGE. By Very Rev. F. Girardey, C.SS.R. 32mo.
  Paper, 0.25; per 100, 12.50; cloth, 0.35; per 100, 21 00
  The instructions treat of the great dignity of matrimony, its indissolubility, the obstacles to it, the evils of mixed marriage, the manner of getting married, and the duties it imposes on the married between each other, and in reference to their offspring.

POPULAR INSTRUCTIONS TO PARENTS on the Bringing Up of Children. By Very Rev. F. Girardey, C.SS.R. 32mo.
  Paper, 0.25; per 100, 12.50; cloth, 0.35; per 100, 21 00
  Contents: The Parental Rights and Obligations; The Two Classes of Parental Duties; Faith and Fear of God; Religious Training at Home; What the Children Should be Taught to Avoid; Devotions which the Parents Should Teach Their Children; Submission to Authority; Purity; The Schooling of Children; Prudence and Tact; Watchfulness; Correction; Good Example; Vocation; Preparation for Marriage; Marriage; Prayers; Appendix.

PRAYER. The Great Means of Obtaining Salvation. Liguori. 32mo, cloth, 0 50

PRAYER-BOOK FOR LENT. 32mo, cloth, 0 50
  Also in finer bindings.

PRAXIS SYNODALIS. Manuale Synodi Diocesanæ ac Provincialis Celebrande. 12mo, *net*, 0 60

PRIEST IN THE PULPIT, THE. A Manual of Homiletics and Catechetics. Schuech-Luebbermann. 8vo, *net*, 1 50

PRIMER FOR CONVERTS, A. Durward. 32mo, flexible cloth, 0 25

PRINCIPLES OF ANTHROPOLOGY AND BIOLOGY. Hughes. 16mo, *net*, 0 75

READING AND THE MIND, WITH SOMETHING TO READ. O'Connor, S.J. 12mo, *net*, 0 50

REASONABLENESS OF CATHOLIC CEREMONIES AND PRACTICES. Burke. 32mo, flexible cloth, 0 35

REGISTRUM BAPTISMORUM. 3,200 registers, 11x16 inches, *net*, 3 50

REGISTRUM MATRIMONIORUM. 3,200 registers, 11x16 inches, *net*, 3 50

RELIGIOUS STATE, THE. By St. Alphonsus de Liguori. 32mo, 0 50

REMINISCENCES OF RT. REV. EDGAR P. WADHAMS, D.D. Walworth. 12mo, illustrated, *net*, 1 00

RIGHTS OF OUR LITTLE ONES; or, First Principles on Education, in Catechetical Form. Conway. 32mo, paper, 0.15; per 100, 9.00. Cloth, 0.25; per 100, 15 00

ROSARY, THE MOST HOLY, in Thirty-one Meditations, Prayers and Examples. Grimm. 32mo, 0 50

ROUND TABLE, A, of the Representative *American* Catholic
Novelists. Containing the best stories by the best writers.
With fine half-tone portraits printed in two colors, bio-
graphical sketches, etc. 12mo, 1 50

ROUND TABLE, A, of the Representative *Irish and English*
Catholic Novelists. The best stories by the best writers.
With fine half-tone portraits in two colors, biographical
sketches, etc. 12mo, 1 50

RUSSO, N., S.J.—De Philosophia Morali Prælectiones in Col-
legio Georgiopolitano Soc. Jes. Anno 1889-90 Habitæ.
8vo, half leather, *net*, 2 00

ST. CHANTAL AND THE FOUNDATION OF THE VISITATION.
Bougaud. 2 vols., 8vo, *net*, 4 00

ST. JOSEPH, OUR ADVOCATE. Huguet. 24mo, 1 00

SACRAMENT OF PENANCE, THE. (Lenten Sermons.) Paper,
net, 0 25

SACRAMENTALS OF THE HOLY CATHOLIC CHURCH, THE. By
Rev. A. A. Lambing, LL.D. Popular edition, illus. 24mo.
Paper, 0.25; 25 copies, 4.25; 50 copies, 7.50; 100 copies, 12 50
Cloth, 0.50; 25 copies, 8.50; 50 copies, 15.00; 1.0 copies, 25 00

" His Eminence is glad that you have brought the work
out at a price which should insure it a large circulation; he
wishes it every success."—Austin Oates, Private Secretary to
Cardinal Vaughan.

SACRED HEART, BOOKS ON THE.

Child's Prayer-Book of the Sacred Heart. Small
32mo, 0 25

Devotions to the Sacred Heart for the first Friday.
Huguet. 32mo, 0 40

Imitation of the Sacred Heart of Jesus. Arnoudt. 16mo,
cloth, 1 25

Little Prayer-Book of the Sacred Heart. Prayers and
Practices of Blessed Margaret Mary Alacoque. Small
32mo, 0 40

Month of the Sacred Heart of Jesus. Huguet. 32mo, 0 75

Month of the Sacred Heart for the Young Christian. By
Brother Phillippe. 32mo. 0 50

New Month of the Sacred Heart. 32mo, 0 40

One and Thirty Days with Blessed Margaret Mary. 32mo,
flexible cloth, 0 25

Pearls from the Casket of the Sacred Heart of Jesus.
32mo, 0 50

Revelations of the Sacred Heart to Blessed Margaret Mary;
and the History of Her Life. Bougaud. 8vo, *net*, 1 50

Sacred Heart Studied in the Sacred Scriptures. Saintrain.
8vo, *net*, 2 00

Six Sermons on Devotion to the Sacred Heart of Jesus.
16mo, *net*, 0 60

Year of the Sacred Heart. 32mo, 0 50

SACRED RHETORIC 12mo, *net*, 0 75

SACRIFICE OF THE MASS WORTHILY CELEBRATED, THE. By
the Rev. Father Chaignon, S.J. Translated by Rt. Rev.
L. de Goesbriand, D.D. 8vo, *net*, 1 50

SACRISTY RITUAL. Rituale Compendiosum, seu Ordo Administrandi quædam Sacramenta et alia officia Ecclesiastica Rite peragendi ex Rituale Romano, novissime edito desumptas. 12mo, flexible, *net*, o 75

SECRET OF SANCTITY, THE. According to St. Francis de Sales and Father Crasset, S.J. 12mo, *net*, 1 oo

SERAPHIC GUIDE. A Manual for the Members of the Third
Order of St. Francis. o 60
Roan, red edges, o 75
The same in German, at the same prices.

SERMONS, Abridged, for all Sundays and Holydays. Liguori.
12mo, *net*, 1 25

SERMONS ON THE BLESSED VIRGIN. McDermott. 16mo, *net*, o 75

SERMONS for the Sundays and Chief Festivals of the Ecclesiastical Year. By Rev. Julius Pottgeisser, S.J. From the German by Rev. James Conway, S.J. 2 vols., 8vo, *net*, 2 50

SERMONS, FUNERAL. 2 vols. 8vo, *net*, 2 oo

SERMONS, LENTEN. 8vo, *net*, 2 oo
See also "Two-Edged Sword" and "Sacrament of Penance."

SERMONS ON MIXED MARRIAGES, EIGHT SHORT. By Rev.
A. A. Lambing. Paper, *net*, o 25

SERMONS, NEW AND OLD. 8 vols., large 8vo, *net*, 16 oo

SERMONS ON THE CHRISTIAN VIRTUES. By the Rev. F.
Hunolt, S.J. Translated by Rev J. Allen, D.D. 2 vols ,
8vo, *net*, 5 oo

SERMONS ON THE DIFFERENT STATES OF LIFE. By Rev. F.
Hunolt, S.J. Translated by Rev. J. Allen, D.D. 2 vols.,
8vo, *net*, 5 oo

SERMONS ON THE SEVEN DEADLY SINS. By Rev. F. Hunolt,
S.J. Translated by Rev. J. Allen, D.D. 2 vols.,
8vo, *net*, 5 oo

SERMONS ON PENANCE By Rev. F. Hunolt, S.J. Translated
by Rev. J. Allen, D.D. 2 vols., 8vo, *net*, 5 oo

SERMONS ON OUR LORD, THE BLESSED VIRGIN, AND THE
SAINTS. By Rev. F. Hunolt, S.J. Translated by Rev. J.
Allen, D.D. 2 vols., 8vo, *net*, 5 oo

SERMONS ON THE MOST HOLY ROSARY. By Rev. M. J.
Frings. 12mo, *net*, 1 oo

SERMONS, SHORT, FOR LOW MASSES. A complete, brief
course of instruction on Christian Doctrine. Schouppe.
12mo, *net*, 1 25

SERMONS, SIX, on Devotion to the Sacred Heart of Jesus.
Bierbaum. 16mo, *net*, o 60

SHORT CONFERENCES ON THE LITTLE OFFICE OF THE
IMMACULATE CONCEPTION. Rainer. 32mo, o 50

SHORT STORIES ON CHRISTIAN DOCTRINE. 12mo, illustrated, *net*, o 75

SEVEN LAST WORDS ON THE CROSS, THE. (Sermons.) Paper.
net, o 25

14

An American Industry. A full description of the Silver-
smith's Art and Ecclesiastical Metalwork as carried on in
Benziger Brothers' Factory of Church Goods, De Kalb
Avenue and Rockwell Place, Brooklyn, N. Y. Small
quarto, 48 pp., with 75 illustrations, printed in two colors.
Mailed gratis on application.

This interesting book gives a full description of the various
arts employed in the manufacture of Church goods, from the
designing and modelling, through the different branches of
casting, spinning, chasing, buffing, gilding, and burnishing.
The numerous beautiful half-tone illustrations show the
machinery and tools used, as well as rich specimens of the
work turned out.

www.ingramcontent.com/pod-product-compliance
Lightning Source LLC
Chambersburg PA
CBHW020121030726

47498CB00006B/2207